AMISH INN MYSTERIES™

Horse *and* Burglary

Virginia Smith

Annie's®

AnniesFiction.com

Books in the Amish Inn Mysteries series

Secrets of the Amish Diary
Plain Deception
Simple Lies
Murder Simply Played
To Love and to Vanish
Law & Old Order
A Silent Betrayal
Humble Pies and White Lies
Deceptive Hearts
Stolen Past
Grave Inheritance
Homespun Homicide
Broken Melody
Horse and Burglary
A Fatal Harvest
A Simple Deduction
The Hound and the Fury
Unhappy Returns
Skating the Law
Book Clubbed
Farmed Robbery
Scene of the Chime
Amish and Old Lace
To Honor and Betray

Library of Congress-in-Publication Data
Horse and Burglary/ by Virginia Smith
p. cm.
I. Title
2017940883

AnniesFiction.com
(800) 282-6643
Amish Inn Mysteries™
Series Creator: Shari Lohner
Series Editor: Jane Haertel
Cover Illustrator: Bob Kayganich

10 11 12 13 14 | Printed in China | 9 8 7 6 5 4 3 2

1

"I hope the baby holds off long enough for us to finish this quilt." Liz Eckardt arched her back, which ached from two hours bent over the quilting frame.

"Hard to tell, since this is Dinah's first." Mary Ann Berne's needle flew with expert speed across the sandwiched quilt. "I think her sister's baby came late."

"I don't know. That was before I moved here." Liz ran a hand over the Churn Dash quilt, one of the first Nine Patch block patterns she'd worked on. She would never have undertaken such a design when she first arrived in Pleasant Creek to open her bed-and-breakfast, the Olde Mansion Inn. However, under the tutelage of the Material Girls—her local quilting group and closest friends—her skills were improving. This pattern was beautiful, and now that the top had been put together, she saw the reason for the name. The arrangement of triangles and rectangles did resemble an old-fashioned butter churn, if she squinted and tilted her head. The pastel colors of green and yellow would be perfect for her Amish cousin's baby, regardless of the gender.

The bell on the front door of the Olde Mansion Inn jingled, and the sound of hurried footsteps echoed across the polished floor.

"Sorry girls." Sadie bustled through the door of Sew Welcome, a bulging bag dangling from her shoulder and a helmet in her hand. "I wanted to ride Penelope today since the weather's nice, but she was acting up. Took me a couple of hours to figure out the problem. Turned out her vacuum line had slipped."

Mary Ann looked up from her work. Twin creases appeared in the smooth skin between her eyes. "I wish you would sell that motorcycle before I worry myself into an ulcer."

Liz wisely held her tongue and returned to her needlework. Mary Ann would have better luck prying a hambone from the jaws of a hungry rottweiler than convincing Sadie to part with her Harley Davidson, appropriately named Pink Penelope.

The older lady halted in the act of dropping her bag on the floor beside her chair. "Are you implying that I'm not a competent motorcyclist?" The words carved through the air like a knife slicing into a Sweet Everything sponge cake.

Not in the least intimidated, Mary Ann maintained her composure. "Well, you *are* in your seventies. How long do you plan to keep riding?"

Eyes flashing, Sadie's chest inflated as she prepared to deliver what would certainly be a blistering reply. Fortunately, the telephone rang in the other room, providing Liz with the perfect excuse to leave before the verbal explosion.

Beans, the English bulldog she'd inherited when she bought the inn, lay sprawled on his favorite rug near the door. He stirred enough to lift an eyelid halfway as she passed on her way to the foyer table. Liz snatched the cordless phone from its charging cradle.

"The Olde Mansion Inn," she said brightly into the receiver. "May I help you?"

A pleasant, deep voice rumbled in her ear. "I hope so. I'm looking for lodging for the weekend. There're three of us, but we don't mind doubling up to save money. I know it's short notice."

September was typically one of the busiest times of the year in Indiana's Amish country, packed with visitors arriving in Pleasant Creek to enjoy the fall weather and the glorious beauty of trees clothed in brilliantly colored foliage. This weekend would draw a big crowd, since the local high school homecoming game would be played on Friday night. Though football was not nearly as enthusiastically celebrated as basketball in Pleasant Creek, between that and the fall weather, the inn had been booked solid for nearly a year.

But as it happened, a wedding party from Shelbyville, Kentucky, had canceled last week after the groom broke his leg in a bicycle accident. A family who had booked a room for the wedding had decided to come anyway. Another room had been snatched up the next day, leaving four rooms available.

"As a matter of fact, I do have something available," Liz told the man.

"Excellent!" Satisfaction colored his tone. "We're a singing group, and we've been on the road for a while performing benefit concerts. Our tenor's voice is shot, and we're all tired. We really need a few days' peace and quiet. Saw your place on the Internet, and it looks like it's just the ticket."

Liz indulged in a smile. She worked hard to keep her website attractive and up to date, and her efforts had paid off in an increasing number of bookings coming from there. "I think you'll find this the perfect place to relax. The inn's grounds are beautiful, and there's a lovely lake right next to us."

"It sounds great. We'll be there tonight, if that's okay."

Most guests checked into the inn on Friday or Saturday, and today was only Wednesday. Already she had one family checking in today, and this group would make two. Now she could recoup some of the money she'd lost due to the wedding party's cancelation. Liz took the man's name and promised to have the rooms ready when he arrived. She jotted a note that the Rose of Sharon Room, the Somewhere in Time Room, the Heirloom Room, and the Sunset Room had been rented, and left it on the kitchen counter where her Amish part-time employee, Sarah Borkholder, would see it.

Another singing group. Liz shook her head. Well, at least there was no singing competition in town this time.

Before leaving the foyer she cast a longing glance toward her private quarters. She'd love to escape to solitude and lose herself in the pages of her current mystery novel. But the quilt for Dinah's baby awaited, and she couldn't leave all the work on this personal piece to the Material Girls. With a wistful sigh, she crossed the rotunda and re-entered the Sew Welcome Shop.

Thankfully, the good-natured battle over the pink Harley had waned, and Sadie sat at the quilting frame, stitching peacefully. Mary Ann was now seated in the far corner reading aloud from the newspaper open in her lap. She had yielded her place to Naomi Mason, who had apparently taken advantage of a lull in business at her bakery, Sweet Everything, that was located next door. Naomi grinned a greeting when Liz entered, but did not interrupt Mary Ann's reading of an article from the *Fort Wayne Times*.

"'We first came across a family living just outside Pristina three years ago,'" Mary Ann read, "'and were shocked by their living conditions. Over the years we have helped them with clothing, food, and wood for the winter, but their actual living conditions have deteriorated. There is no one to offer aid. So, small as we are, we have undertaken to help them and families like them improve their situation. We will have a lot of fund-raising to do over the next six or eight months, but we can't just walk away and let the children go hungry.'" She clucked her tongue, compassion displayed in the creases that gathered on her forehead.

"What charity is that?" Naomi asked.

Mary Ann scanned the paper. "A small group that organized a few years ago to help needy families in Kosovo. Never heard of it, but it's registered and tax deductible."

Liz slid into her seat and picked up her needle. "Maybe we should make a quilt for them and donate the proceeds."

Sadie looked up from her stitching. "I like that idea. We could do a Christmas theme and raffle it off."

Nodding, Mary Ann lifted the newspaper slightly. "I bet if we contact the reporter who wrote this article she'll help us advertise."

"Good idea." Sadie nodded to indicate the matter was settled. "That's our next project then."

And a good one too. Liz shifted on her chair to achieve a comfortable position, and bent to her sewing. With each stitch she built a mental image of a tiny baby with Dinah's pert nose and bow lips. Warmth gathered in the vicinity of her heart. This baby would be loved and, though he or she would live in simple Amish surroundings, would never know need. There would always be plenty to eat and warm clothing in the winter, and a huge circle of love wherever it went.

Mary Ann interrupted Liz's thoughts. "Well, I would never have thought this could happen."

"What's that?" Sadie asked without missing a stitch.

"Somebody robbed Fort Knox."

"How in the world did they manage that?" Though Liz had never been to Fort Knox, she had a vague mental image of bricks of gold piled to the ceiling in huge vaults. "Gold is heavy. They'd have to use a wheelbarrow or wagon or something, wouldn't they?"

"It's not just gold there anymore. There's a cache of opium and morphine that was stored up during the Cold War, and other valuable items are frequently stored there on a temporary basis. What did the thief steal?" Naomi asked as she tightened her stitch with care.

"The article doesn't say—only that the official statement was released confirming that a theft had been committed." Mary Ann scanned the article. "They suspect an inside job involving multiple people. Civilians." She glanced up. "I didn't know they employed civilians at Fort Knox. Since it's an Army base, I would have thought it was all Army guys there."

Sadie clucked her tongue and shook her head. "What's the world coming to, when the military has to hire Tom, Dick, and Harry to work for them?"

Swallowing a chuckle, Liz managed an even tone. "I doubt if they pull people off the streets. Surely they put them through some sort of vetting and training process."

"Hmph." Sadie's grimace spoke volumes.

Thankfully, Mary Ann turned a page and interrupted what might have become a tirade. "Girls, here's an article that says gasoline prices are going to rise, maybe as early as tomorrow." She glanced around at her friends. "We'd better fill up our cars tonight."

Sadie straightened. "Another reason why I should ride Penelope as long as the weather cooperates. She gets over fifty miles to the gallon."

Liz exchanged a quick glance with Naomi and then ducked her head, but not before seeing Mary Ann's normally serene face tighten into a faint scowl. Stitching continued in silence for several long moments, which spoke well of Mary Ann's ability to put a clamp on her tongue.

"Oh my gracious!"

Work on the quilt ceased as Liz and the others stopped mid-stitch to stare at Mary Ann. "What's wrong?" Liz asked, faintly alarmed at the suddenly white-faced shock on her friend's face.

"Spit it out, girl," Sadie commanded.

Liz was in the process of rising to go to the woman's side when Mary Ann delivered the news.

"Louise Younger has been murdered!"

2

Work on the quilt ceased while everyone turned stunned looks toward Mary Ann. Though the name meant nothing to Liz, any murder was horrifying. She knew that from personal experience.

"Who is—was—Louise Younger?" she asked.

"She used to live in Pleasant Creek, right?" Naomi tucked a chocolate-brown curl behind her ear. "She left before I moved here, but I've heard her name mentioned."

"Louise was a friend," Sadie told them. "She lived two doors down from Mary Ann, and they were close."

Liz's heart wrenched when she saw Mary Ann trying to read the newspaper while blinking away tears. She left her chair to retrieve a box of tissues from beneath the register counter.

"I'm so sorry." She offered one to her friend. "Does the article say what happened?"

Blotting at watery eyes, Mary Ann sniffed. "Apparently she surprised a robber in her house and was stabbed. That was three weeks ago." She lifted a troubled gaze to Sadie. "I don't remember seeing an obituary. We would certainly have gone to the service. We only have this because it announces her estate sale."

"Of course we would've." Sadie's features darkened. "That no-good nephew of hers probably didn't even have a funeral for her."

"But she has a sister-in-law in California, or used to." Mary Ann shook her head. "I haven't talked to Louise in several months. I should have stayed in touch better."

"Maybe the service was held out there." Liz pulled her smartphone out of her pocket and opened an Internet browser. She typed *Louise Younger obituary* into the search bar. "You said she lived in Fort Wayne?"

Dabbing at her eyes, Mary Ann nodded.

"There's no newspaper obituary listed, but I found an entry on a website." She scanned the page. "They don't say much, only that she was seventy-one years old and passed away on August 27. Oh, here it is. "'A memorial service will be held at two o'clock on September fifteenth at the First United Community Church in Oakdale, California.'"

"That was last week." Mary Ann plucked another tissue from the box to absorb a fresh wave of tears. "We could have sent flowers if we'd known."

With a sniffle, she returned to the newspaper while Sadie retrieved her quilting needle and made a few vicious stabs at the fabric. "Robbery? Huh! I'll bet that nephew of hers killed her."

Liz raised an eyebrow at Naomi, who shrugged.

"Sadie, be nice." A hint of Mary Ann's traditional calm manner returned. "Gavin caused a lot of trouble, and poor Louise took the brunt of the fallout, but he loved his aunt. He would never harm her."

"Hmph!" The older woman's glower showed what she thought of her friend's opinion.

Curiosity got the best of Liz. "What kind of trouble did her nephew get into?"

"You name it, that boy did it." The creases around Sadie's lips deepened. "His mother unloaded him on Louise because she couldn't handle him. He shoplifted candy bars from the drugstore and pulled tricks that were just plain mean, like unscrewing the tops of the salt shakers at the Burger Heaven. And he painted graffiti all over the clock tower."

"Nobody ever proved he was the culprit," Mary Ann corrected.

"It was him all right. Everybody knew it." Sadie's lips twisted even further. "For some reason, Louise doted on the boy, probably because he was her dead brother's only child. Even bought him a car when he graduated high school. Why, a body wasn't safe on the streets until the day he left town."

"Why did they move to Fort Wayne?" Naomi asked pausing to rethread her needle.

Sadie and Mary Ann exchanged a loaded look, which piqued Liz's curiosity. Sadie opened her mouth to answer, but Mary Ann cut her off.

"Let's just say he and a local girl got involved, and her family didn't appreciate the negative influence. Louise was so ashamed at the rumors and accusations being spread—even though most of them weren't true—that she couldn't show her face. Started going out of town for groceries and such." Shining silver hair swayed as she shook her head, sorrow heavy on her features. "I tried to talk her out of moving, but she insisted she needed a fresh start." A sigh. "I suppose she did."

Ever kind and gracious, Mary Ann must have had a reason for not wanting to go into the details. She glanced across the quilt stand at Sadie, who wore her disapproval like a Halloween mask. Liz hid a grin. Later she'd get Sadie alone. It wouldn't take much prying to get details from that source.

"The article says Louise's house and belongings are being sold at auction tomorrow." Mary Ann folded the newspaper, rose, and laid it in her chair. "I think I'll go. Maybe I'll pick up a memento to remember her by."

"And put money in Gavin's pocket?" Sadie blew a raspberry. "He'll not get a cent from me."

"Nor from me. The paper said she left instructions in her will that all proceeds from the sale of her estate be given to a local no-kill animal shelter."

Even Sadie seemed surprised at that news. "Gavin must have done something pretty awful to get himself cut out of her will."

Naomi clipped her thread. "I wish I could go, but I don't have anyone to cover the bakery then. Speaking of which, I'd better get back." She stooped to pick up her purse before rising from the chair. "I'll see you later."

Liz glanced at the clock. Her guests would begin arriving soon, and it wasn't fair to let Sarah do all the work in the inn. "Me too." She rose and then paused to glance over the beautiful baby quilt. "I think this one is my favorite so far."

Sadie laughed. "You say that about every quilt we make."

That was true, but there was something special about this one. She ran a hand over the soft fabric and pictured it wrapped around a sweet-smelling bundle of joy. This quilt represented the promise of a new life born into her own family, and she'd sewn every stitch with love.

The first of her guests arrived just as Liz slid a batch of cookies onto a wire rack to cool. The aroma of warm chocolate followed her from the kitchen to the rotunda.

She opened the front door and smiled brightly at the trio standing on the porch. "Welcome. You must be the Porters. I'm Liz Eckardt. Please come in."

The hand she extended was shaken by a middle-aged man with a moon-shaped face, and then crushed in the strong grip of a thin woman whose smile flashed into her eyes.

"Eunice." The woman jerked her head toward her husband as they carried their luggage into the rotunda. "He's Otis. And this is our son, Caleb."

Liz tilted her head back to examine Caleb, whose lanky height caught her by surprise. "When you mentioned on the phone that your son needed to stay in the same room with you, I made the assumption he was younger. And, uh, *shorter.*" She aimed a smile up at the young man. "The pull-out sofa bed may not be long enough for someone as tall as you."

Caleb turned an indignant expression toward his mother. "We're sharing a room?"

Patting his arm, an indulgent simper slid over Eunice's face and her tone became annoyingly high-pitched, as though talking to a toddler. "I want to be able to keep an eye on my baby boy. What if you need something during the night?"

"Mother, I can get my own drink of water. I'm eighteen years old."

"Barely." Eunice explained to Liz, "His birthday was last week."

Otis stepped to her side. "Now, son, don't argue. Mother knows best."

A pained look came over the boy's face and he opened his mouth, but then closed it again without replying. Resignation settled on his features, which sent a jolt of sympathy through Liz. Though she'd known the Porters less than five minutes, the family dynamics were crystal clear. Poor Caleb had been born to a pair of helicopter parents. A lifetime of being hovered over had taught him that he had no choice but to comply with their wishes.

Well, Liz could offer a small gesture in the matter of the rooms.

"Actually, I'm afraid I've had to rearrange the accommodations." She kept her tone pleasant while looking Eunice directly in the eye. "The room with the fold-out couch has been assigned to another guest. So I'm actually relieved your son is older, since I have no choice but to put him in one of the smaller single rooms on the third floor."

Deep creases appeared in Eunice's forehead. "But we reserved that room months ago."

"I know, and I'm truly sorry for the mix-up. As compensation I'll discount the nightly rate by twenty percent." The woman's head started to shake, and Liz hurried on. "And of course there will be no charge for the second room, since the mistake was mine."

Otis's expression brightened, but Eunice continued to frown.

"What about a rollaway bed? Don't you have one of those Caleb could sleep on?"

From the corner of her eye Liz saw the young man tense.

"I'm afraid not." She poured apology into her tone. "I've been meaning to purchase a few to keep on hand, but I haven't gotten around to it yet. But let me assure you, the Rose of Sharon Room is one of the house's nicest, and has a beautiful view of the lake. I'm sure you'll be comfortable there. Caleb will be directly above you, and the stairs to the third floor are right outside your door."

"I'll be fine, Mother. And right upstairs."

Eunice's lips twisted into a crooked line. "It appears we have no choice."

Guilt for her deception niggled at Liz, but a quick glance toward Caleb eased her conscience. He was clearly relieved. Besides, the singing group representative said they didn't mind doubling up. She could install two of them in the Heirloom Room and save them a bit of money. Business had been good recently, so she could afford to be generous for a couple of days.

"Thank you for understanding." Before either Eunice or Otis could reply, she continued. "I wanted to ask how the groom is doing with his broken leg. I understand he's your relative?"

"The son of Otis's cousin, twice removed," Eunice replied.

"Boy's doing as well as can be expected." Otis shook his head. "Terrible situation, that."

"Yes, very sad. I understand he was in a bicycle accident?"

"Mowed down by a car." Otis scowled. "Driver never even stopped. Hit and run."

"That's terrible." Liz hadn't heard the details. The bride's mother had been understandably upset and distracted when she called. "I hope he'll recover soon. If you'll follow me, I'll show you to your rooms."

"Hey, you have a dog," Caleb said. Beans was snoozing on his rug.

"That's Beans," Liz said, "the laziest canine the world has ever seen."

"Is it okay to pet him?"

Before she could say, "Sure," Eunice spoke. "Don't touch it, baby. Your hands will stink."

As though he'd heard and understood, Beans uttered a sleepy grumble.

Liz laughed. "Beans doesn't smell bad. He may be lazy, but at least he stands still for baths." As if to prove a point, she stooped and rubbed the dog behind one ear, ending with a pat on the head. The dog made sounds of contentment, but didn't wake.

A struggle appeared briefly on Caleb's face, but instead of following suit he tightened his grip on the handle of his suitcase.

What is the matter with me? Liz rose and led the way through the rotunda and up the stairs. She'd acted purposefully in defiance of Eunice's directive, and even felt the prickle of disappointment when Caleb didn't follow suit. Shame on her for undermining the woman in front of her son! But Eunice's overprotectiveness grated against her nerves. Thank goodness Liz had raised her godson, Steve, to be independent and make his own decisions. She'd taken him in after her good friends, his parents, had died when he was seven. He now served in the military in Kosovo, and she couldn't be prouder of him.

But who was to say her approach to child-rearing was the best? If Eunice wanted to hover over her son it was none of her business. When the young man finally grew weary of being smothered, he would stand up for himself on his own.

Eunice and Otis were pleased with the Rose of Sharon Room and exclaimed over the beautiful view, as well as the white vintage furniture, and the prints of delicate flower and bird photos by Gene Stratton-Porter. Eunice even dropped her nose into the colorful bouquet of orange and yellow giant marigolds, clearly pleased with the gesture of fresh flowers in the room even though marigolds were not known for their pretty scent. Thank goodness they were pleased with the room. Liz let go of her guilt and led Caleb—with Eunice following—up to the third floor.

"Here you go." She smiled at the young man as she twisted the handle and swung the door inward. "We call this the Sunset Room because it faces west, so you have a beautiful view of the sunset."

The decor in this room was not nearly as quaint and feminine as the one where the older Porters would stay, but in Liz's opinion it was more conducive to rest. It featured a mix of modern and antique furnishings, with white walls and brightly colored art and cushions that mirrored the brilliant colors of the sunset.

She indicated a closed door down the hallway with a nod. "The bathroom is there, and you'll find plenty of hangers in the closet if you have anything that needs to be hung up."

For a moment Liz feared Eunice would insist on occupying the other guest room on this level to be close to her "baby boy." But her desire to give the young man a few nights' privacy succeeded. Neither of Caleb's parents asked about the nearby Sunrise Room.

"Baby, put your bag there." Eunice pointed toward the floor in front of a plain but attractive chest of drawers. "I'll unpack for you."

Caleb did as he was told, and Liz bit her tongue. No doubt Mother did all his laundry for him and had probably even packed the suitcase. When the poor kid finally managed to break away, he would have a lot to learn about living on his own.

"When you've gotten settled in, I'll be happy to give you a tour of the house." Before she left them alone, Liz added, "We have coffee-and-cookie hour every afternoon, a chance for guests to relax and get to know each other."

"That sounds delightful." Eunice unzipped the luggage. "Caleb loves cookies."

Liz smiled. "Double chocolate tonight."

With a goodbye smile, she exited and descended the stairs. Teenage boys, even smothered ones, shared a universal trait—their stomachs were perpetually empty. When Steve was Caleb's age she'd been unable to keep food in the house, especially cookies. Maybe she should bake another batch.

Eunice directed a mildly disapproving stare toward her son as he reached for his fourth cookie. "Now, baby, don't fill up on sweets. We're going to a nice restaurant for dinner."

The sitting room felt even cozier with a fire flickering in the fireplace, the first one Liz had lit this fall. Indiana could be smothering in the summer, and Liz had missed being able to use the inn's fireplaces. Beans obviously approved, since he had stirred himself enough to waddle from his rug to the hearth, where he resumed his afternoon nap. His soft snore blended with the crackle of burning wood and gave the room a satisfactorily homey atmosphere.

Caleb grinned and took a bite. "Don't worry, Mother. I'll eat dinner."

Eunice sipped from her coffee mug and turned to Liz with an indulgent smile. "He will too."

"A bottomless pit," Otis announced as he, too, leaned forward to snatch another cookie. "And not an ounce of fat on him." He held his coffee mug beneath his chin and dunked the treat.

The smile on his wife's face melted. "If you keep eating like that you won't be able to say the same. You're not eighteen anymore."

Instead of being offended, as Liz certainly would have been, Otis settled back on the sofa, bit into the coffee-soaked cookie, and then heaved a satisfied sigh. "If you baked like Ms. Eckardt, I'd have a spare tire around my middle for sure."

The doorbell interrupted whatever response Eunice might have made. Glad for the excuse to leave, Liz set her coffee on the end table and rose. "Excuse me while I check these guests in."

Three men stood on the porch, each carrying a small overnight bag. Liz welcomed them with a smile. "Mr. Pulliam?" She looked into each face.

The tallest of the trio held out a hand, and spoke in the friendly voice she'd heard on the phone. "That'd be me, ma'am. You can call me Maddox." He gestured toward the short, thin man on his right. "This is Donnie Higgins, and that's Phil Chesser."

She shook hands with each in turn, noting that Donnie's solemn expression might almost be described as a scowl, and Phil did not quite meet her eyes. Maddox was definitely the most outgoing of the group. "I'm Liz Eckardt."

"We appreciate you fitting us in on such short notice." Maddox lifted his head to sweep over the inn. "You've got a beautiful place here. I'm surprised you had room for us."

"Normally I wouldn't have, but a wedding party canceled yesterday."

"Not cold feet, I hope." He indulged in a laugh, though his friends remained stone-faced.

"The groom had an accident." She saw no reason to elaborate, and instead looked around the porch. "Do you want to bring your instruments inside?"

Maddox answered her question with a blank stare. "Instruments?"

"Since you're a music group I assumed you'd have instruments." She craned her neck to look for their vehicle. The wide driveway contained two cars, neither big enough to carry much in the way of musical equipment.

Phil spoke for the first time, his words short and clipped. "No instruments. We sing."

"Just voices," Donnie supplied.

"That's right." Maddox's wide smile returned. "I must not have mentioned that on the phone."

"How wonderful. Maybe you'll entertain us one afternoon during coffee-and-cookie hour." Although she seriously doubted they could be as good as the barbershop quartet who'd stayed there recently.

Donnie opened his mouth, a protest plain on his face, but Maddox cut him off.

"Maybe, but like I said, we're hoping to rest our voices for a few days. Phil here is starting to get a scratchy throat from all the gigs we've had lately."

He had mentioned that on the phone.

"Then I'd best not keep you standing on the porch." She opened the door and gestured for them to enter. When they were all inside she crossed to the small reception desk and slid the registration pad toward them, talking as she did so. "You mentioned earlier that you were interested in saving money by doubling up. I only have one room with two beds, and one of them is a fold-out sofa. I've arranged for you to have that and one other." She peered at Phil, the shortest of the three, who should sleep quite comfortably on the sofa bed.

"Yeah, yeah, that's fine," Maddox assured her. "Gotta save money wherever we can."

"Then if you'll just give me your credit card, I'll—"

"We'll pay cash." Donnie made the statement in the loud, flat tone of one who expected an argument. Liz arched her eyebrows, and he lowered his gaze, shamefaced. "We just came from a gig and they paid us in cash. That's okay, isn't it?"

"Cash is always acceptable."

She jotted down the price for the Heirloom Room and the Somewhere in Time Room, added the appropriate taxes, and extended the receipt. While Maddox completed the registration form, Donnie whipped out a worn leather wallet and carefully counted out a stack of bills.

The business portion of check-in taken care of, Liz led them through the rotunda and up the gleaming curved staircase. As expected, Phil claimed the sofa, and Maddox took possession of the comfortable Heirloom Room bed. That left Donnie in the Somewhere in Time Room, with its dozens of clocks and beautiful old pine floor. Liz interpreted his grunt as satisfaction.

She indicated the Rose of Sharon Room. "There's a couple staying there, and their son is upstairs. Tomorrow a guest is arriving to stay there." She pointed toward the Amish Room.

"We'll be so quiet no one will even know we're here," Maddox promised.

"As I mentioned downstairs, every afternoon I serve coffee and cookies in the sitting room. It's a chance for the guests to relax and get to know one another." She glanced at her watch. "It's almost over now, but the Porters' son might have left some cookies if you're hungry."

"We just ate," Phil said.

Though surprised at the man's abrupt manners, Liz merely nodded. Was he rude, or merely awkward around strangers? A stain appeared on his cheeks, confirming her suspicions. *Awkward, definitely.*

"But maybe we'll join you tomorrow," Maddox said.

"I would enjoy that." She directed her comment to Maddox, but aimed an extra-wide smile at Phil to put him at ease. "Breakfast will be served at seven thirty in the morning. Normally I'm flexible on the timing, but tomorrow I'm going to an auction in Fort Wayne."

He brightened. "What kind of auction?"

"The estate of a woman who used to live here in Pleasant Creek." Liz shrugged. "I'm guessing there will be a mishmash of stuff, household odds and ends."

"I like auctions. Maybe I'll go along." He exchanged a glance with Phil, who was staring at him.

The lines cleared from Phil's forehead and he straightened. "Yeah, me too. I like auctions."

Donnie shrugged. "Might as well. We don't have anything else planned."

"I'll get you the address," Liz told them. "Or you can follow my friends and me. We plan to leave here around eight thirty."

"Sounds good."

"I'll leave you to get settled in." On her way to the stairs, she spoke over her shoulder. "If you need anything at all, please don't hesitate to ask. My quarters are downstairs near the kitchen."

When she reached the first landing, she glanced upward to see Maddox and Phil disappear into the Heirloom Room. Donnie had not moved, but stood watching her descent. A shadow from the open door fell across his face, turning his eyes into dark holes. When she looked up, he jerked as though she'd caught him at some mischief, gave her a bashful smile, and hurried into his room.

How in the world did a shy man like that manage to sing in public? Maddox must be the group's spokesman, both onstage and off. Though both Donnie and Phil seemed pleasant enough, neither possessed Maddox's outgoing nature.

She'd love to hear them, even just one song, to see how they measured up to the other groups she'd hosted at the inn. Maybe after Phil's voice had rested for a day or two, they'd consider a brief performance during coffee hour.

At the bottom of the stairs, Beans stood on his squatty legs, watching her with an unmistakable expression on his doggy face.

Liz laughed. "Looks like somebody's ready for his supper."

When she reached the floor she stooped to rub his ears. "Come on, lazybones. Let's go get something to eat."

On the way to the kitchen, she sniffed her fingers. Though she hated to admit that Eunice might be right, perhaps it was time for Beans to have a bath.

3

"In a quarter mile, turn right onto Stowe Street, then your destination is on the right."

The aristocratic voice of her GPS, whom she fondly called Lavinia, flowed from the cell phone. Liz braked as her Acura approached the street, and Lavinia offered a reminder. "Turn right."

From the back seat, Sadie asked, "How do they get all the streets in the whole country programmed into that thing?"

Mary Ann turned her head to answer. "Don't think about it. It'll give you a headache."

"Your destination is on the right."

"She has a way of stating the obvious, doesn't she?"

Liz smiled at Sadie's remark as she scanned the street for a place to park. The auction had transformed what appeared to be a quiet neighborhood into something resembling the parking lot of a shopping mall at Christmastime. Cars lined both sides of the narrow avenue, and a steady stream of auction-goers flowed in the direction of a small house midway down the street. She slowed as they drew near.

"I may have to go around the corner to find a parking place. Why don't you two get out here and I'll join you in a minute?"

Mary Ann turned a smile her way. "How sweet. Thank you."

The pair climbed out of the car and joined the throng that swarmed past the house into the backyard. As she continued down the street, Liz glanced at the rearview mirror. Maddox waved from behind the steering wheel of his car.

At the end of the street she found an empty space on the right and flipped on her blinker. The car passed her and turned the corner up ahead while she backed into the slot. A memory brought a smile to her face. The first time Steve attempted parallel parking after receiving his learner's permit, he'd been so focused on not hitting the car in front that he tapped the one behind. Thankfully there had been no damage to either car, but he'd battled what he considered "unmanly tears" all the way home.

The task accomplished, Liz grabbed her purse and exited the car. They had half an hour before the auction started. Plenty of time to look around and see if there was anything she wanted to bid on.

She followed a middle-aged couple around the side of Louise Younger's neat little house. The lawn had been set up like a yard sale, with items covering the surfaces of several rows of folding tables. The door to a screened porch stood open, and people streamed in and out of the house.

A hand waving above the heads of the milling crowd drew her attention, and she spied Sadie and Mary Ann near a detached garage.

"Find anything to bid on?" she asked as she joined them.

"Not much." Sadie said. "And with a turnout like this the prices are going to be high."

"I saw a quilt I'd like to have," Mary Ann said.

Sadie laughed. "Like you need another quilt."

"Louise and I worked on it together." A faraway look rose in her eyes. "It has sentimental value."

A stack of paint cans in the garage drew Liz's attention. She stepped around her friends and lifted one by the metal handle. "This is full. Maybe she was getting ready to do some painting."

Mary Ann bent to inspect the splash on the lid. "That creamy beige is a nice, neutral color."

"My quarters could use a fresh coat of paint," Liz said. "And this color would brighten Sew Welcome's walls too."

"It *has* been a while since we painted in there," Mary Ann agreed.

"Folks, we're gonna get started here in about ten minutes."

The voice, issuing through a loudspeaker, drew their attention to the far corner of the yard, where a platform had been erected. A red-faced man in a suit stood behind a table, a gavel in one hand and a microphone in the other.

"Goodness, it's getting crowded out here," Sadie said as people filed out of the house, filling the small backyard to near capacity.

On the far side of the crowd Liz caught sight of her musical guests. She gave a little wave, which Maddox returned.

Mary Ann's head swiveled as she scanned the crowd. "I was sure Gavin would be here. I wonder where he is."

"Probably in jail somewhere," Sadie said cheerfully.

The auctioneer described the process and how bidders needed to register and obtain a numbered bidding card.

"I think I'll do that." Liz turned an inquisitive look on her friends. "What about you?"

Mary Ann nodded. "Definitely."

"Not me. What do I want with somebody else's junk when I've got plenty of my own?" Sadie shrugged. "Besides, if I see something I can't live without, I'll get one of you to buy it for me."

They made their way to the registration table.

"The next item up for bid is a steamer trunk," the auctioneer announced. "Now folks, it might look a touch shabby, but you know these old trunks fetch a pretty penny when they're cleaned up a bit. And they're built to last."

Sadie leaned sideways to whisper into Liz's ear. "He's right about that. I've seen them on that public television show about antiques."

Liz inspected the trunk from her vantage point at the front of the crowd. The hardware had blackened with age, and the leather handle on the nearest side was stretched and worn. The auctioneer instructed his assistant to lift the lid, and Liz craned her neck to peer inside at the aged paper lining.

"What am I bid for this trunk?" His gaze swept the onlookers. "Who'll start the bid at one hundred dollars?"

A mumble rippled around the yard, but no one volunteered a bid. The auctioneer conceded. "All right then. Let everybody in." He began the familiar singsong chant. "Who'll give seventy-five? Seventy-five, seventy-five? Who'll give seventy-five right now?"

Someone behind Liz shouted, "Twenty-five!"

The man pointed his gavel. "I have twenty-five, twenty-five, who'll give thirty? Twenty-five, gimme thirty."

Words rippled across his tongue, stirring Liz's excitement. The trunk would look lovely if refinished, and would fit perfectly in the Heirloom Room. That hardware was probably brass. A bit of polish would bring out the shine. She bit her lower lip and glanced toward the pile of items she'd already bought. A mismatched pair of vintage lamps, tarnished but still functional, would fit perfectly with the decor in the third-floor guest rooms. The five gallons of paint had gone for a song, less than two dollars each. But whatever had possessed her to buy the elevated dog-bowl shelf? Beans didn't care if he had to bend his neck to eat—he wasn't very tall in the first place, and he would put up with just about anything for food. The box of DVDs would be added to the collection from which she allowed her guests to borrow, but what in the world would she do with the two dozen plastic napkin rings?

"Thirty!" came the auctioneer's triumphant call. "I've got thirty, now who'll give me forty? Thirty, gimme forty. Thirty, gimme forty."

"Forty!" Liz waved her bidder's card in the air.

Mary Ann raised an eyebrow, but Sadie nodded approval.

"Forty, gimme fifty. Forty, gimme fifty."

"Forty-two," called the man behind her.

Liz hid a smile and cast a glance over her shoulder. Her competition was slowing down. No way was she letting that chest go for a pittance. "Forty-five!" she shouted.

The auctioneer didn't even have time to reply before the man's voice behind her countered. "Forty-seven!"

She whirled and scanned the faces behind her through narrowed eyelids. "Fifty!" she called toward the front while daring anyone behind her to speak.

He didn't.

"Fifty dollars going once." During the pause Liz drew in a breath and held it. "Going twice." Silence. "Sold for fifty dollars to the pretty lady down front."

Satisfied, Liz smiled at her friends. Then she grasped each of them by an arm and whispered frantically, "Now get me out of here before I do any more damage."

Laughter ringing, Mary Ann steered her out of the crowd. Maddox and the others had apparently lost interest in the auction at some point because they were nowhere to be seen. When Liz had settled her account with the cashier, she recruited a couple of hefty-looking men to help haul their purchases to the sidewalk. Mary Ann's quilt fit into the steamer trunk along with the pair of framed prints she'd bought for Sadie.

"Whatever possessed you to buy that thing?" Sadie pointed at the dog feeder.

"Possessed is exactly the right word." Liz fished the keys out of her purse. Sadie was usually all for spoiling Beans. If *she* questioned the purchase, Liz felt ridiculous. "I don't know what came over me."

Mary Ann patted her shoulder. "Well, it was for a good cause."

"You two guard our stuff while I get the car. I hope that trunk fits in the trunk." Chuckling at the play on words, Liz headed down the sidewalk.

A few minutes later, when she glided the Acura to a stop in front of Louise's house, a young man stood talking with her friends. No, *talking* was not an accurate description. He was shouting, his face red and his arms waving wildly around his head. She shoved the gearshift into park and hurried toward the sidewalk.

Sadie fixed an unreadable stare on her, while Mary Ann said calmly, "Here's Liz now."

The young man whirled and thrust a finger at her, barely an inch from her nose. "It's mine, I tell you! Aunt Louise told me I could have it. Give it back right now."

4

His finger stabbed at her, the scent of stale cigarette smoke assaulting her nostrils. Apparently Louise's nephew had decided to put in an appearance after all.

Liz drew herself up and adopted her sternest tone. After all, she'd been a lawyer in Boston for years. "Don't raise your voice to me, young man. I won't tolerate being shouted at."

With a visible effort, he withdrew his finger and drew in a shuddering breath, though the angry red stain on his face did not dissipate. "I'm sorry," he ground out through clenched teeth. "But my aunt promised. And I bought that paint myself. I was going to come up and paint her walls for her."

Sadie eyed the young man. "If she intended you to have anything, why didn't she leave it to you in her will?"

"That's a good question, Gavin." The look Mary Ann gave him was kinder. "The paper said she left instructions that everything should be sold and the money given to the animal shelter."

His eyes snapped sideways, and he ran his fingers roughly through curly brown hair. "That was a misunderstanding. I got into some trouble a few months ago, and she cut me off. But we got past that, and we were good when she died. She said she was going to change her will, but I guess she didn't have time."

He fell silent. The grief that twisted his features looked genuine. Sympathy stirred in Liz's heart.

Sadie narrowed her eyes. "If there's something you wanted so badly, why didn't you get here in time to bid for it?"

"I tried! I had to drive up here from Kentucky and got stuck in construction traffic." He faced Liz. "I'm sorry I lost my temper. Really. Would you consider selling me the stuff you bought?"

This time the apology did sound genuine. Liz studied him. He was a handsome young man, with sparkling blue eyes offset by a head full of thick curls.

"What is it you want?" She glanced at the items piled on the grass beside her.

"Well, all of it. I mean, I kept my stuff in that trunk when I lived here, and one of those lamps was in my bedroom. I'll buy it all from you and give you double what you paid."

Actually, now that the excitement of the auction was wearing off, she was able to look at her purchases with a clearer head. The dog feeder and napkin rings had been ridiculous purchases, and really, what did she need with that old trunk? And though the lamps would look nice in the Sunrise and Sunset Rooms, both already had plenty of lighting. If they meant that much to this poor young man who had lost his aunt, why shouldn't he have them?

Before she could open her mouth, Sadie stepped behind Gavin and fixed Liz with a hard stare. She shook her head vigorously and mouthed, "No." Liz glanced toward Mary Ann, and saw her give a very slight shake of her head as well. *Interesting.* Her friends had known both Louise and Gavin, and neither thought he should have these items.

She arranged her lips into an apologetic smile. "I'm sorry, but I'm keeping them."

His jaw hardened, and his hands clenched into fists. But he merely gave a single nod, and then whirled toward the house. Without a word, he strode around the corner and into the backyard.

When he had gone, she turned to her friends. "Why didn't you think I should let him have them?"

"Because he doesn't deserve them," said Sadie.

Mary Ann tilted her head, staring in the direction Gavin had gone. "I don't know about that, but I can't help thinking if Louise had wanted him to have them, she would have given them to him before now. That trunk might be old enough to be valuable. And Gavin has never struck me as a sentimental person."

Liz eyed the trunk. Mary Ann was right. He probably wanted it so he could sell it and make a pile of money. "I still feel bad for him. Maybe he just hasn't been able to get up here if he lives in Kentucky. After all, she *was* his guardian." Like she'd been Steve's.

Mary Ann looped an arm through hers. "Don't give it another thought. If he wants something to remember her by, there are still plenty of things left to bid on. Now let's get this stuff in the car and go get some lunch."

Liz stepped back and admired the lamp. It looked perfect in the Sunset Room, as she had known it would. The white alabaster base contained a dark marbling that gave it a vintage look, though she suspected it wasn't as old as it appeared. She'd probably replace the lampshade, though. The scalloped chandelier-style shade had appeared creamy yellow in the sunlight, but here it looked a bit shabby. If she kept her eyes open, she'd find a lampshade that suited the room's decor better. This would do in the meantime.

Gathering the bedsheets she'd just replaced, she headed downstairs to start a load of laundry.

"Liz, do you have a minute?" Mary Ann called to her from Sew Welcome.

"Sure." She dropped her bundle on the washing machine in the utility room and then went to the shop.

"We're trying to decide on the edging of our Christmas quilt." Mary Ann gestured toward the craft table. "What do you think?"

Fabric swatches had been arranged on the surface, dozens of brightly dressed snowmen surrounded by a forest of patchwork evergreens. One edge consisted of a green checked pattern, and the other was of a more subdued tan speckle.

Sadie tapped on the tan material. "I think this one makes it look like a rug more than a quilt. Tell her, Liz."

Liz inspected both, then nodded. "I don't know about a rug, but I like the green better. The colors offset the trees and really make the snowmen pop."

"Okay, I concede." Mary Ann rolled the rejected fabric around the bolt and returned it to the shelf.

Liz lingered before returning to her chores. "I can't stop thinking about Gavin. I wonder if he bought anything at the auction."

Sadie didn't say anything, but slipped into her chair by the quilt stand, where the baby quilt was nearing completion.

"You're feeling guilty, aren't you?" Mary Ann asked.

Nodding, Liz sank against the edge of the table. "I know it's silly, but I keep comparing him to Steve. If anything happened to me, Steve would be devastated."

Mary Ann patted her hand. "Louise and Gavin didn't have the same kind of relationship as you and Steve. She doted on him, true, but I never felt like he appreciated her as much as he should have."

"She's right." Sadie plied her needle. "He took advantage of her. I know I've said it before, but it still wouldn't surprise me if he's the one who killed her."

Liz was surprised when Mary Ann gave a shamefaced nod. "Honestly, after Sadie planted the seed in my head, I've wondered the same thing."

Silence fell between them for a moment, broken when Mary Ann straightened. "I'm sure we're wrong. I've been looking through newspapers from the past few weeks, and it appears the police have questioned several suspects, though of course the police won't release names."

Sadie tilted her head thoughtfully. "You'd think if her own nephew was a suspect, the papers would have found out somehow and be all over that."

"Exactly. The last statement made by the police is that the robbery was probably a random burglary, and they're still asking for anyone who might have information to come forward." But a shadow of doubt lingered around her eyes.

"Do you think Gavin is capable of murder?" Liz asked quietly.

Neither woman answered at first, but then Mary Ann shook her head slowly. "I don't *want* to think so."

"He certainly caused a lot of trouble when he was here," Sadie said, "but he was never violent."

Could the young man she'd met that morning be a ruthless killer? He certainly didn't have the look of a murderer. Of course, murderers came in all shapes and sizes, as she well knew.

"What would be his motive?" she asked. "Louise wrote him out of her will. He would gain nothing from her death."

"That's true." Looking relieved, Mary Ann began to gather fabric samples from the table.

"Then I'm going for the random robbery theory. But if he did kill her the police will figure it out," Sadie said. "Unless we decide to get involved."

Liz was trying to come up with a response when a voice echoed to them from the rotunda. "Hello?"

"That must be my final guest." Liz pushed herself upright from the table and left the shop.

In the rotunda stood a stout woman dressed in brown polyester slacks and a gray raincoat. Her eyebrows had been penciled on in a pair of unfortunate arches that gave her a perplexed expression. A purse dangled from one forearm, and draped along the length of the other was a black-and-white cat.

"Hello. Sorry, I didn't hear you come in. I'm Liz Eckardt, the innkeeper. Are you Ms. Lewis?"

"I am, but please call me Betty." She craned her neck to look around the rotunda, wavy dark hair with a liberal sprinkling of gray flying freely around her head. "What a beautiful room. So elegant."

"Thank you." Liz extended a hand toward the cat. "And who do we have here?"

Full lips spread in a proud smile. "This is Frank." She lifted her arms to nuzzle the feline with a cheek. "He's named after my dear father, God rest his soul."

Frank regarded her hand with amber eyes that narrowed slightly. Liz stopped just short of touching him. He didn't look as though he would enjoy being petted.

"I didn't realize you were bringing a cat."

"I never go anywhere without Frank." Betty's eyes widened. "Your website said you allow small pets."

The website also stated that guests should notify her of any pets when making a reservation. Since it was too late now, Liz didn't mention that. "It's fine. I hope Frank doesn't mind dogs."

They both turned toward the foyer, where Beans lay in his usual place.

"Frank *adores* dogs."

To prove it, Betty marched toward the snoozing bulldog and set the cat on the floor directly in front of Beans's nose. Frank stood in place while Beans's nostrils twitched. He lifted his head and raised brown doggy eyes to Liz, then settled his gaze again on the cat. As though oblivious to the canine's presence, Frank seated himself, raised a paw in the air, and began licking his armpit.

"See?" Betty beamed at the animals. "They'll be best friends by the end of the day. Now, if you don't mind I'd like to rest after the drive. Would you have the porter bring my luggage to my room?"

Liz noted three old-fashioned hard-shell suitcases beside the door.

"I don't have a porter, but I'll be happy to help." She reached for the biggest suitcase and gasped when she lifted it. What did the woman have in there, bricks?

"Thank you. I assume the guest accommodations are upstairs?"

Without waiting for an answer, and without taking any of her own luggage, Betty swept from the foyer in the direction of the stairway. Struggling to carry the heavy suitcase, Liz started to follow. A movement drew her gaze just in time to see Frank draw back a paw and slap Beans's face with a set of wicked-looking claws. The dog yelped and retreated into the corner, while the cat sauntered after its owner.

"Oh!" Liz dropped the suitcase and hurried to kneel at the bulldog's side. Whimpering, he ducked his head and pawed at two long scratches on his wrinkly jowl. "Poor Beans. Let me settle her in her room and then I'll get some disinfectant to clean those scratches."

She scowled after the cat. *Adores dogs, my foot!*

5

"These are delicious, Ms. Eckardt." Maddox finished off an oatmeal raisin cookie and reached for a second.

"Thank you, and please call me Liz." She included the others with a gaze that swept the room and then settled on Eunice Porter. "Did you have a pleasant day?"

Seated on the sofa between her husband and son, the woman beamed. "Wonderful! We rode in an authentic Amish buggy and saw a group of children dressed in Amish costumes. So adorable."

Liz hid a smile. How would her cousin Miriam react if she heard her conservative dress described as a *costume*?

"And you?" Liz directed her question to Donnie, who had accepted coffee but refused the offer of a cookie.

"We did some hiking in the woods down on the other side of the lake. Pretty country hereabouts."

"It was a beautiful afternoon for a hike." She looked at Phil. "How are you feeling?"

He stared at her, his expression blank.

"Your throat. I hope it isn't causing you too much discomfort."

"Oh, that." He raised a hand to his throat. "It's still kind of scratchy, but it doesn't hurt." His gaze flickered toward Maddox. "Much."

Footsteps in the rotunda preceded Betty, who swept into the room with Frank in her arms. "Goodness, I slept like the dead!"

An hour ago Liz had taken clean sheets and towels up to the linen closet and heard proof that the claim was true. The woman snored like a chain saw.

"I hope you find the room comfortable." Liz stood and offered her chair to Betty, and then crossed the room to get a clean coffee mug.

"It's wonderful." Settled in the chair with Frank in her lap, she eyed the single-cup coffee maker. "Do you have decaf?"

Liz checked the rack. "Not here, but I'll get some from the kitchen if you'd like."

"Please. If I drink regular this late I'd be awake all night. Especially after my long nap."

She leaned forward for a cookie. Apparently Frank didn't appreciate being squashed in her lap, because he hopped down and sat at her feet. When he did so Beans, who had been snoozing on the hearth, raised his head. He watched the feline with what looked like caution. Liz didn't blame him a bit.

"Please introduce yourselves. I'll be back in a minute with that decaf."

When she returned with a handful of individual pods of decaf coffee, Betty had taken command of the conversation.

"I do some singing myself. I've been a member of the church choir for over twenty years." She accepted the mug from the tray Liz held and waved away the offer of cream and sugar. "First soprano."

Eunice looked at Phil. "What a shame you're not feeling well. I would love to hear you."

"Do you have a CD?" Otis asked.

Donnie and Phil exchanged a glance, and Maddox shook his head. "We haven't been together very long."

"Yeah," Donnie agreed. "We're just getting started, really."

Eunice set her cup on the table. "What's the name of your group?"

No one answered at first, and Liz intercepted a quick glance between Phil and Donnie. Maddox finally broke the silence. "We call ourselves the Three Eagles."

Phil jerked upright, and the look he turned on Maddox could only be described as angry. That surprised Liz. Why would he be angry if the others knew their group's name? A suspicious niggle itched in the back of her mind.

A laugh blasted from Otis. "Had to put that Three on the front so you weren't confused with the more famous band, eh?"

Smiling, Maddox agreed.

"What parts do you sing? No wait! Let me guess." Betty tilted her head and eyed Donnie. "You're a tenor." She pointed at Maddox. "And you're a bass, which must mean you—" She looked toward Phil. "Are the baritone."

Maddox smiled. "You know your voices."

"As I said, I've been singing a long time." She settled back in the chair. "Name some of the songs in your repertoire."

With an abrupt movement, Donnie jumped out of his chair. "I hate to be rude, but I'm so hungry my stomach is starting to sing its own song."

His music partners stood as well.

"We're thinking of trying that Italian restaurant on the north end of town." Maddox looked at Liz. "Do you recommend it?"

"Pasta Heaven?" She nodded. "Try the Blissful Lasagna. It's delicious."

Turning to Caleb, who was chewing his fifth cookie, Eunice spoke in the high-pitched tone she reserved especially for him. "Caleb loves lasagna, don't you, baby?"

The teenager maintained a bland expression, though he sighed as he nodded.

She looked at Otis, and her voice dropped an octave. "Let's go there for supper."

"Fine with me." He slapped his hands on his thighs and heaved himself off the couch.

"You will be here tomorrow evening, won't you?" Betty asked. "My brother, Benjamin, is renting a cabin at Crystal Lake this week, and I hope he'll join us for coffee hour tomorrow." She turned to Liz. "If that's agreeable to you, of course."

Liz waved a hand. "Certainly."

The smile on Maddox's face widened. "We'd love to meet your brother."

Something in his tone caught Liz's attention. The words sounded exaggerated, as if he meant the exact opposite. But why? She gave her head a quick shake. Maybe he found Betty's bragging about her own singing and her questions annoying.

When the six had left, Liz resettled herself in the chair facing Betty's. "I enjoy coffee hour. It's a time for me to get to know my guests better."

"Quite pleasant," she agreed. "You must have a full house this week."

Liz's coffee had cooled. She set the mug on a coaster. "Almost. I was supposed to, but I had a cancelation. There's one vacant room up on the third floor." A single cookie sat on the tray amid a smattering of crumbs. Liz gestured toward it. "Why don't you have that last one?"

"I might as well." She leaned forward and snatched it up. "Do you have a restaurant recommendation besides Italian?"

"There's a very good café called Mama's Home Cooking."

"I passed it on the way here this afternoon. That sounds more to my taste." She patted her generous middle. "Spicy sauces give me a sour stomach."

An easy silence fell as she munched her cookie. Beans, who had lain back down, kept a wary watch on the cat instead of returning to his nap. When Frank rose and walked with a graceful step toward the hearth, Beans jerked upright into a sitting position, his body tense.

"Oh look." Betty beamed at her pet. "Frank wants to make friends."

Sure enough, the feline approached Beans. Instead of growling or leaving, as Liz expected, Beans remained statue-still. Though it looked like Frank might pass him, at the last minute the cat leaned in and rubbed up against Beans, then turned and rubbed him with his other side.

Betty laid a hand on her chest. "Isn't that the sweetest thing?"

It certainly looked as if Frank had undergone an attitude change from this afternoon. Perhaps he'd only been tired, like his owner. Some of the stiffness left Beans's limbs as the cat made its way around to his other side and repeated the rubbing there. Well, he'd always been an amiable dog when it came to other animals.

The doorbell chimed. Liz excused herself to answer it.

When she swung the door open, she froze as statue-still as Beans. On the front porch stood Gavin, a small duffel bag slung over one shoulder.

"Bet you're surprised to see me."

Shocked is more like it. "I certainly wasn't expecting you."

"I came to apologize for my behavior this morning. I was upset because I'd missed the first part of the auction, and because . . ." He ducked his head. "Well, I haven't been myself since Aunt Louise was killed. I can't stop thinking about it. It was so sudden."

A twinge of sympathy struck her. To have a loved one die a violent death would certainly haunt a person.

Especially if he killed her himself.

The conversation with the Material Girls came back to her, and her grip on the door handle tightened.

"I understand," she said, "and I accept your apology."

"Thank you." A boyish grin appeared on his face. "Actually, I have another reason for coming."

Here it came. "If you're going to try to convince me to sell you that trunk—"

"No ma'am." He raised a hand with three fingers extended. "Scout's honor."

Thank goodness. Even though Mary Ann and Sadie insisted she had no reason to feel guilty, she hadn't been able to shake the idea that she should have at least given him the lamp that had been on his bedside table.

"I picked up a newspaper this afternoon and found out that Pleasant Creek High School's homecoming game is tomorrow tonight. I haven't been back to town since . . ." He bit a lip. "Well, since Aunt Louise and I moved. I think I'll go. Who knows, I might even run into some of my old friends and teachers."

From what Sadie had said about Gavin, there probably weren't many of his teachers who would be pleased to see him again. But Liz said, "That would be nice."

A sad expression settled on his face, and his shoulders sagged. "I just drove by our old house. The one where I lived with Aunt Louise. It looks . . . the same."

The sympathy in Liz's chest ballooned. This young man might have been a delinquent as a teenager, but she had no doubt he loved his aunt.

Footsteps behind her alerted her to Betty's approach. She turned to find her guest carrying the coffee tray loaded with dirty cups and crumpled napkins.

"I'll take these to the kitchen if you'll tell me where it is."

"Please don't trouble yourself." Liz moved to take the tray from her. "You're a guest here. You don't have to clean up."

She set the tray on the entry hall table and turned back to find that Gavin had left the porch and now stood in the foyer.

"I'm sorry to interrupt." Betty waved toward the duffel bag. "Looks like you're about to fill that vacant room."

"No," Liz said quickly. "This is, uh, a friend of a friend. Not a guest."

Gavin took a step forward, his expression eager. "Actually, that's what I was about to say. The other reason I came here is to see if you had any vacancies. I need a place to stay for a few days if I'm going to the ball game."

"What good fortune for both of you." Betty clapped her hands. "Now you really do have a full house, my dear."

Liz opened her mouth but then closed it again, her protest unspoken. If only Betty had not come into the room just then, she could have claimed that there was no room at the inn. A lie, of course, and one that would probably haunt her. The young man had lost a loved one. How could Liz turn him away when he was feeling nostalgic about the town he had lived in with his late aunt?

But what if he *murdered her?*

No. She didn't believe that. What possible reason would he have for killing Louise? He gained nothing from her death. In fact, if his story was true and Louise planned to change her will to include him, he'd lost everything he might one day have inherited.

But if he *did* know anything about his aunt's murder, having him here would provide Liz an opportunity to pry the information out of him.

Pasting on a smile, she stepped around him and shut the front door. "Welcome to the Olde Mansion Inn. I do require payment in advance."

"Sure, no problem."

She led him to the reception desk and handed him the registration pad. What would Sadie say when she discovered Gavin was staying at the inn? Liz suppressed a shudder.

When Gavin had been installed in the Sunrise Room, Liz returned to the sitting room to tidy up and tend the fire. Betty had gone upstairs to get her coat. Liz rounded the corner in time to see Frank execute an acrobatic leap from the back of an upholstered wing chair to the fireplace mantel.

"Hey! You come down from there."

The cat ignored her and proceeded to wind in and out of the knickknacks resting on the ledge. He came to a stop directly over Beans. The bulldog sat with his head cocked back to watch the activity above him.

"Go on, shoo!"

She started across the floor, but before she could reach him, Frank wedged himself behind a framed photograph. With a sideways thrust, the cat shoved the frame off the mantel. Liz gasped as the picture came crashing down—directly onto Beans's upturned face.

Poor Beans let out a yelp and raced from the room, nearly knocking Liz over in his haste to escape.

She turned back to the cat. "You did that on purpose, you mean thing."

Amber eyes focused on her, and then Frank jumped down from the mantel and strolled regally from the room, his tail in the air.

6

Friday morning breakfast was served in shifts. The Three Eagles arrived in the dining room at eight, and the Porters soon after. Betty had advised Liz the night before that she preferred to sleep in today, and apparently so did Gavin. When the first shift left the table, Liz took the remaining apple cinnamon muffins and a bowl of fruit salad back to the kitchen to seal them for the latecomers.

When she entered the room, she was surprised to find not one, but two Amish women there.

Sarah was already working on the dishes. "*Guta morgan.*" Her black *Kapp* dipped in a nod, her arms up to the elbows in soapy water in the sink.

"Good morning." Liz turned a smile on the young woman seated at the table before a steaming mug. She looked vaguely familiar. "Hello. I'm Liz Eckardt."

Sarah half turned from the sink. "This is my friend, Anna Beachy. Isaac had to take our *Valga* in to have the wheels looked at, so Anna brought me to work."

"*Hallo.*" A shy smile curled the edges of Anna's lips.

Liz held out the half-full basket of muffins. "Would you like one? They're still a bit warm."

"*Dänka*, but no. *Mutter* and my sisters and I cooked a big *Stümorga.*"

"What you call breakfast," Sarah explained when Liz looked confused. Liz smiled gratefully. She knew some Amish words, but not all.

When the fruit salad had been deposited into the fridge, Liz slid open a drawer and extracted a roll of plastic wrap. "I'm going to leave these muffins out for a bit. Two of our guests are sleeping in."

When all the dishes had been retrieved from the dining room and stacked beside the sink for Sarah to wash, Liz picked up a towel and joined her. When Sarah was off, Liz used the dishwasher, but Sarah preferred the manual method.

Beans sauntered into the room and went to the corner where his bowls were kept. A creature of habit, the dog had not been pleased by the appearance of the shelf that raised his bowls off the ground. Though Liz was sure he would eventually accept the new arrangement, he approached his breakfast with a long-suffering grumble.

"Get used to it," Liz told him. "Eating from an elevated bowl is healthier for you. I looked it up on the Internet."

A snort issued from his scrunched nose before he began to eat.

"Is that true?" Sarah asked.

Liz dropped her voice to a whisper. "Who knows? I paid good money for it though, and he might as well use it."

Sarah and Anna giggled.

"We picked up another guest last night. I put him up in the Sunrise Room," Liz said at regular volume. She stacked the dry plates in the cabinet. "Gavin Younger."

The muffin tin Sarah was rinsing clattered back into the sink. Her normally sweet features darkened.

The conversation with Mary Ann and Sadie replayed in Liz's mind. If only she'd known more details about the situation, she might have been able to come up with a good reason not to give him a room.

"I'm sorry." Liz poured sincerity into her tone. "He's upstairs already. Did you know him?"

"Not personally, but I know about him."

"Everybody does," said Anna. "He is not a nice boy."

"He is *vëschta*." Sarah scowled. "Very bad."

The two nodded. Liz folded the towel and draped it across the sink. Sarah never said an unkind word about anyone. Gavin must have done something terrible to garner such a judgment from her.

She folded her arms across her chest and leaned against the counter. "Tell me."

The young woman hesitated, her eyebrows drawn together.

Anna spoke up. "He drew Leah Schwartz away. Convinced her to leave her family, her *church*."

"Leah Schwartz." Liz scanned the list of Schwartzes she knew. "Is she related to Viola Schwartz?"

"Her daughter." Sarah dried her hands on her apron. "Everyone tried to convince Leah not to leave. Even after, they wrote letters to her in Kentucky, where she went with *him*."

"My sister was her friend. She wrote several times," Anna said. "Leah never answered. Viola and Asa and the bishop went to visit, to convince her to return, but she wouldn't talk to them. They came home heartbroken."

Liz saw the situation clearly. Gavin, the troublemaking *Englisch* boy, had gotten romantically involved with an Amish girl and convinced her to leave the Amish church, which would devastate her entire close-knit community. No wonder Mary Ann didn't want to speak of it. Viola and Mary Ann were friends. Viola didn't quilt, but Liz had met her several times when she shopped for dress fabric in Sew Welcome.

If only Liz could ask him to leave. But Lawyer Liz kicked in. She'd rented the room to Gavin for three nights and had accepted payment in advance. Evicting him based on past behavior was out of the question.

"I wish I'd known before." Liz took Sarah's hands. "I wouldn't have let him stay, I promise. But I can't force him to leave now."

Tears welled in Sarah's green eyes, whether from sorrow or anger Liz couldn't tell.

"But you don't have to clean up after him." She squeezed the still-damp hands. "I'll take care of the Sunrise Room. In fact, you don't have to see him at all. If you'd rather leave now, you can. By the time you come back to work on Monday he'll be gone."

With a sniff, Sarah held her chin high. "I will stay. I won't leave all the work to you."

A deep voice from the doorway interrupted. "Uh, excuse me?"

For one horrified moment Liz thought Gavin had come down for breakfast, and a confrontation was imminent. Instead, she turned to see Caleb's hulking frame in the doorway.

"Hello." She released Sarah's hands and turned a bright smile on the boy. "Did you need something?"

"Well, uh." His gaze circled the room, flitted across Sarah and landed on Anna. A flush colored his cheeks. He wrenched it away and looked back at Liz. "Uh, I was just checking to see if there were any of those muffins left."

Liz hid a smile. The bottomless pit of a teenage boy struck again. "Certainly." She picked up the basket, peeled back the plastic wrap and extended it toward him. "Take as many as you like."

While he helped himself to three muffins, she performed the introductions. "Caleb Porter, this is Sarah Borkholder, who helps me here at the inn. And her friend, Anna Beachy."

His blush deepened as he ducked a nod at Anna, and then a quicker one in Sarah's direction. "I'm gonna eat these out by the lake, if that's okay."

Out of the probing gaze of his mother?

"Of course. The door through there will take you right out beside it." She pointed him in the direction of the four-season room.

He balanced the three muffins in one large hand and helped himself to another. Then with a long-legged stride he left the room.

"I'm about to dirty some more dishes," Liz told Sarah with a laugh, breaking the tension. "I need to whip up another batch of muffins."

Liz opened her laptop, pressed the power button, and waited for the computer to boot up. Something about the Three Eagles bothered her. Maddox was friendly enough and seemed completely genuine. But the looks she kept intercepting between Phil and Donnie left her unsettled.

Her gaze fell on Louise Younger's trunk. She'd placed it against the far wall in her quarters. It looked dingy and out of place. Her enthusiasm for the thing had dimmed after the encounter with Gavin. Though she'd originally intended it for the Heirloom Room, now that she'd stared at it for a while, she didn't think it would fit there. Maybe when it was cleaned up she'd be able to find an appropriate place for it, but now she couldn't picture it in any room in the house.

Beside the trunk, the five cans of paint formed an incomplete pyramid. They mocked her, taunting her with the thought that she should get busy and use them. But what a chore. She'd have to take everything off the walls and cover all the furniture before she could even begin the actual work of painting. Besides, she was booked almost solid for months—what if she started the job, but then didn't have time to finish it? She could have partially painted walls for months. She turned her back on the cans.

Sunlight sparkled on the smooth surface of the lake outside her window. Today promised to be mild and warmer than usual for mid-September. Good weather for tonight's homecoming game. Her thoughts followed a trail that led to Gavin, then to Leah Schwartz. Liz's own mother had left the Amish, though for a different reason than Leah. When Liz had first arrived in Pleasant Creek, she didn't realize what a devastating effect such an action inflicted on those left behind. Now she enjoyed a relationship with her Amish relatives and understood more about what a departure from such a close-knit community of faith meant to them. No wonder Sarah's emotions had run high when Gavin's name was mentioned.

Activity outside the window drew her from her thoughts. Liz watched Anna exit the inn. Before turning to the driveway where her horse and buggy waited, she caught sight of Caleb seated on the bench in the gazebo. The young man jumped to his feet at her approach. The two exchanged a few words, and then Anna settled herself on the bench, tilting her head to speak with Caleb. After a moment, he too perched on the opposite end of the bench but remained ramrod straight, his movements jerky.

Liz indulged in a smile. At that age Steve had been awkward around girls too.

Her computer fully powered on, Liz opened a browser and typed *three eagles* in the search bar. A list appeared, various businesses with names including the term, but no singing groups. She added the word *trio*. Nothing. Then she tried *three eagles music*. The results included videos of several singing groups, but her guests were not among them.

The suspicious niggling intensified. Surely there would be *some* mention of the group tucked into the vastness of the Internet. On a list of performances at an event, for instance.

Closing the laptop's lid, she left her desk. Though she respected the privacy of all her guests, she couldn't in good conscience leave a mystery like this unresolved.

As she entered the rotunda, Phil stepped off the staircase. He brightened when he caught sight of her. "Hello again."

Careful to keep her expression pleasant, she gestured toward his jacket. "Are you heading out?"

"Yes. The others are already in the car, but I left my phone up in the room." He held it up to show her. "We're going to check out the marina, and maybe do a little fishing."

"That will be nice. Before you leave, may I ask you something?"

He shrugged. "Sure."

How to pose her question without sounding like an accusation? She decided on a mostly direct approach. "I was hoping you might have some demo songs online, and I wanted to hear your music so I searched for your group on the Internet. I didn't find any listings for the Three Eagles."

Was that guilt that flickered onto his face? Or fear? "Uh, we've talked about building a website, but we haven't gotten around to it yet. Like we said last night, we're still pretty new at this."

She conceded the point, but continued to watch him closely. "A good website will do wonders for your business. I can attest to that."

He hesitated, his gaze averted. Then he raised his head and looked her directly in the eye. "To be honest, we're not very good. The others aren't bad. I'm definitely the weak link."

The confession appeared to be sincere. Liz detected no falsehood in his expression, and found her sympathies stirred by his hangdog posture. "Surely that's not so."

"It's the truth," he answered with a vigorous nod. "I don't have a musical ear like the others." He lowered his voice as if sharing a secret. "In fact, my throat really isn't scratchy. I messed up this last performance so badly I was embarrassed and made up the sore throat as an excuse. I'm trying to work up the courage to tell Maddox I want to quit."

That explained the secretive glances. He'd probably already confided in Donnie, but hadn't broken the news yet to the group's leader.

The front door opened and Maddox appeared in the foyer. "There you are. Are you coming?"

"Yeah, sure."

Phil gave Liz a loaded look, and she smiled her assurance. His secret was safe with her.

When the two had left, she wandered into Sew Welcome to find Mary Ann, Sadie, and her cousin, Miriam, hard at work on the baby quilt.

Miriam lifted a smile. "Good news. Dinah's birthing pains started in the night. The precious *Bubby* should arrive today."

"How exciting!" Liz inspected the quilt. The three had made amazing progress. The edging was half finished. "I'll help after I've seen to the guest rooms."

A voice alerted her to Gavin's presence a second before he entered the shop. "Have I missed breakfast?"

In the moment before she whirled, she saw her friends' eyes go wide.

"Of course not," she told him. "Just give me a moment to pull it together."

He cast a charming smile at the women working on the quilt. "Surprised to see me again so soon?"

Sadie's jaw dangled, while Miriam, whose face had gone white beneath her Kapp, ducked her head low over her work.

Mary Ann found her voice. "Why, yes. I am. What are you doing here, Gavin?"

Her gaze slid to Liz, who wanted to cringe. If only she'd had time to warn them. Though Miriam presented only the top of her Kapp, the fabric trembled in her fingers.

"I decided since I'd made the trip all the way up here, I might as well stay the weekend. Go to the game tonight, and maybe look up some old friends."

"I'm sure you have plenty of friends left in Pleasant Creek," Sadie said in a voice that confirmed she meant no such thing.

Liz jumped in before Gavin could respond. "Uh, I'll serve you in the dining room."

He hesitated, his gaze circling those in the room. Then he gave a pleasant nod and left.

Liz turned back toward her friends. "I'm sorry. He showed up last night, and I felt sorry for him."

"Sorry?" Miriam's head jerked up. "For *him*?"

Immediately on the defensive, Liz cast a hurt look at Mary Ann. "Well I didn't know about Leah Schwartz until this morning. Otherwise I never would have let him stay."

At the mention of the girl's name, a pained expression overtook Miriam's features. She bent again to her needlework.

"Of course you wouldn't have." Mary Ann reached up to pat Liz's arm. "I should have told you."

Feeling slightly better, Liz turned toward the kitchen to get Gavin's breakfast.

"No good will come of this. You mark my words." Sadie's dire prediction followed her from the room.

7

"Thank you for a delicious breakfast." Betty dabbed her mouth with a napkin and then set it on her empty plate. "I think I'll take a drive to enjoy the fall colors. The countryside in this area is so lovely."

Liz picked up the plate. "That sounds like a nice outing. Have a good time."

Full lips drew into a pout. "I wish my brother would come with me, but he says he's not interested. I can't imagine why he'd suggest that I come to Pleasant Creek for the weekend if he didn't plan to spend time with me." She heaved a sigh. "But at least he agreed to come to coffee hour this afternoon, and then we're going to dinner tonight."

"I look forward to meeting him." Liz had no intention of commenting on sibling conflict. She'd already stirred up enough trouble for one weekend.

Sarah had begun cleaning the guest rooms, so Liz stacked the last of the breakfast dishes in the dishwasher. When the dining room was clean and restored to order, she headed toward the stairs to tackle the third-floor rooms. Entering the rotunda, she spied a black-and-white tail disappearing around the corner of the foyer. Betty had left Frank free to roam the house.

Could animals have split personalities? At times Frank seemed as sweet as could be, sitting demurely at his owner's feet, or purring and winding in and out of her legs. Other times he acted like a possessed creature. Liz had caught him sharpening his claws on the decorative rug in the sitting room, and when she scolded him, he hissed at her. He seemed to particularly enjoy tormenting poor Beans.

The dog was in his favorite lounging spot on the rug in the foyer. What was that cat doing? Liz headed in that direction and stepped through the entryway in time to see a blur leap from the surface of the desk—*her* desk! The glass lamp that rested on the corner crashed to the floor at the same time Frank landed on Beans's back.

Taken unawares mid-snore, Beans shot to his feet with a howl. Frank hung on, his claws digging into the dog's skin. Beans dashed past Liz, yipping pitifully, while Frank bounced like a cowboy on the back of a bull. With a quick glance at the shattered glass, she whirled and chased after them.

"Beans! Stop!"

The terrified animal dashed through the rotunda and into the kitchen. Liz caught up with him in the four-season room, running in circles in his attempt to dislodge a hissing Frank. She leaped for them and made a grab for the cat. On her third try, her fingers finally found fur.

"Got you."

As if she'd thrown a switch, Frank's hissing stopped. Needle-like claws retracted, and he went limp in her hands. With one terrorized glance upward, Beans raced from the room.

"You are a demon," she told the cat, who had the audacity to purr.

Holding tightly, she marched up the stairs. The door to the Amish Room had been left ajar, probably so Frank could access his litter box. She set him in the center of the guest room floor.

"Now you behave, you hear? No sharpening your claws on that quilt."

Frank curled his tail around his feet and began cleaning himself, acting for all the world as if he had not just rained terror downstairs. Liz shut the door and went to check on poor Beans.

The Porters didn't return in time for coffee hour. Liz eyed the three dozen snickerdoodles piled on the cookie tray. Maybe she'd leave a plate in the Sunset Room for Caleb to enjoy when they returned.

She would not do the same for Gavin, who had opted to grab an early dinner somewhere before the football game and therefore was also absent.

The day had been warm enough that she really didn't need a fire this evening, but Beans enjoyed warming himself on the hearth in any weather. He'd had such a traumatic day Liz built a fire just for him. He lay there, soaking in the heat, the tiny claw-shaped sores on his back barely discernable from the antibacterial ointment she'd applied.

However, her other guests were present, and Betty's brother was there as well. Benjamin Baggett proved to be his sister's complete opposite, both in build and demeanor. While Betty engaged the Three Eagles in animated conversation, the bone-thin man sat stiffly in a wing chair and viewed the others from beneath a heavily lined brow.

"And I found the most beautiful Adirondack chairs outside a furniture store not far from here." Betty slurped her coffee. "If I had room in my car I would have bought a pair."

"I know the owner," Liz volunteered, an image of Pleasant Creek's handsome mayor, Jackson Cross, rising in her mind. "He ships."

The woman smiled. "Well, I might have to pay him a visit tomorrow."

Maddox had selected the chair facing Benjamin's. "So what do you do, Ben?"

The man's glower deepened, and Betty hurried to correct Maddox. "He prefers Benjamin. Our grandfather was called Ben." She looked at Liz and confided, "He was an unpleasant man."

"*Benjamin*, then." Maddox flashed his trademark grin.

At first it looked as though Benjamin wouldn't speak, but then he uttered a grudging answer. "I'm between jobs at the moment."

Betty supplied the details. "He worked for the same company for over ten years, but they didn't appreciate him." She leaned over to pat his leg. "Benjamin is taking a well-deserved break before looking for an employer who recognizes the true value of his skills."

Maddox's smile widened. "I wish you luck and fortune."

Benjamin's eyes narrowed, and his silence threatened to become awkward. Liz raised her coffee cup and studied him over the rim. An odd man. Something about him seemed familiar. She did detect the resemblance to his sister, but that wasn't enough to make her think she'd seen him before.

Phil cleared his throat. "Betty told us you're up here fishing. We gave it a try today but hardly got a nibble."

"You having any luck?" Donnie asked.

"A little." Benjamin shrugged, but did not elaborate.

Another silence descended, but before it became awkward, Frank glided into the room. Though Liz assumed Beans was deeply asleep, the moment the cat appeared he leaped to his feet and scurried away. He carved a wide path around Frank, who ignored him.

The cat passed Liz, approached his owner's legs and began to weave in and out.

"How long have you been here?" Donnie addressed his question to Benjamin.

"'Bout a week."

"And are you planning a lengthy visit?" Maddox asked.

In answer, he received another shrug.

Well that solved the riddle of why he looked familiar. If he'd been here a week, she'd no doubt seen him around town.

Frank left Betty's legs and began the same feline dance around Benjamin's.

"Oh look," she exclaimed in an indulgent, pet-loving voice. "He remembers you."

There was no mistaking the scowl he aimed down at the cat.

When Betty took a sip from her coffee mug, the man lifted a foot and shoved the cat away. Liz hid a smile. He might be taciturn enough to border on rudeness, but she couldn't fault someone for disliking that cat.

Betty picked up a magazine and held it at arm's length. "I've left my glasses in my room. Excuse me for a moment, please." She set her mug on the table and hefted herself out of the chair.

Liz followed her into the rotunda. "Betty, may I have a word in private?"

The woman turned halfway across the floor. "Of course, dear."

Liz set her features in a pleasant but professional expression. Oh, how she hated confrontations, but sometimes they went with the job. "I'm afraid I'm going to have to charge you for a lamp Frank broke today. The one in the foyer."

The woman's eyes went round. "Whatever do you mean? Frank isn't destructive. Maybe that dog of yours knocked it off."

That dog of yours? With an effort, Liz managed to keep a polite smile in place. "I saw it with my own eyes. And he knocked a photograph off the mantel last night, but thankfully that didn't break." *Only because it landed on Beans's face.* "From now on, I'll have to ask you to either take him with you when you leave, or close him in your room."

She could mention his tormenting of Beans, but decided against it.

Betty's sputtering was interrupted by the ringing of the telephone.

"Excuse me." Liz made a hasty exit and reached the phone on the third ring. "The Olde Mansion Inn. How may I help you?"

"I'd like to speak to Gavin Younger." A male voice on the other end held enough gravel to pave a driveway.

Liz hesitated. Rarely did she receive a call for a guest on the business phone. Everyone carried a cell phone these days. She'd seen

Gavin's clipped to his belt. Besides, she had an obligation to protect the identity of her guests.

"I'm sorry, but there's no one here by that name." A true statement, at least for the moment.

Now the voice became gruff. "I know he's staying there. He told me so himself."

Something in the man's manner scraped across her nerves like sandpaper. "If you have another number for him, I suggest you call that one."

"He's not answering. I need to leave a message."

She remained silent. To agree would be to confirm his presence. That, she wouldn't do.

"Tell him to call Joe. And he'd better call tonight."

A click, and the line went dead. Liz stood still while a chill crept up her spine. The menace in the message had been unmistakable. She was being asked to relay a threat.

But a threat of what?

"It's a boy!" Mary Ann beamed at Liz, keys jingling as she unlocked the door to Sew Welcome the next morning. "I just ran into Tabitha Miller at the market, which is why I'm late opening up. She said Dinah and the little one are doing great."

"A boy." Liz grinned. Dinah's husband, Seth, must be proud enough to burst his suspenders.

"I called Sadie, and we'd like to pay a visit this afternoon. It will only take us a couple of hours to put the finishing touches on the quilt."

"So soon? Will Dinah be up to visitors?"

Mary Ann waved the concern away. "Tabitha said she's already up and eager to show off her son. But we won't stay long. Can you get away for an hour or so to go with us?"

As if she'd let them have all the fun of bestowing their gift without her. "Definitely. And I'll be down to help finish the quilt as soon as I get the guest rooms settled."

"Excellent." With a wave, she entered the shop.

Liz made her way upstairs. The Porters and the Three Eagles had already eaten breakfast and left for their daily activities. She passed the second-floor landing and saw Sarah bustling around cleaning the Rose of Sharon Room, where the older Porters were staying. Liz would start on Caleb's room upstairs.

At the top landing she encountered Gavin standing in front of the Sunset Room, his hand on the doorknob.

What in the world was going on here?

"Can I help you find something?" she asked.

He jerked upright and whirled. When he saw her, color drained from his face. "Uh, n-no. Oh, wow. This isn't my room." He gave a short laugh. "Sorry about that. Got turned around."

His expression shouted, *I'm lying*!

Liz held her polite smile in place and pointed down the hall. "Your room is there."

"Yeah, it sure is. My mistake." He raked fingers through his hair. "They look alike, and the plaques on them both start with *Sun*. Besides, I had kind of a rough night. A little too much to drink. Guess I'm kind of foggy this morning."

Though sorely tempted to express her disapproval of drunkenness, Liz held her tongue while he edged sideways down the hall toward his own room.

As his hand twisted the knob, she asked. "Did you get the message I left on your door?"

"Uh, yeah." Again, his hand scrubbed at his scalp. "Thanks."

"The man was quite insistent that you return the call last night."

"I did." He opened the door. "Hey, listen, don't bother with breakfast for me. I'll grab a donut from next door or something." With the manner of someone escaping, he disappeared into his room and shut the door.

Liz approached the Sunset Room and tried the knob. It turned. The next time she saw Caleb she would caution him about locking his door.

Inside, she paused and let her gaze circle the room. Everything seemed to be in order. Caleb was a neat young man and even made his own bed. A pair of folded pajamas rested on the pillow. The empty cookie plate from last night sat on the bedside table.

Then her gaze fell on the alabaster lamp. A deep suspicion came over her. Was Gavin entering or leaving the room when she saw him? She had the impression he was leaving, but maybe she'd interrupted him on his way in. Was he planning to steal his aunt's lamp?

8

Her chores finished, Liz dropped by the foyer to check on Beans. He snoozed in his regular spot, but not with his usual abandon. At the sound of her entry, he jerked upright. Recognizing her, he settled back down, but kept a watchful eye on the doorway.

"How are you doing, boy?"

She dropped down on her haunches to give his ears a good rub. Even that failed to relax him, the poor thing. She checked his injuries, relieved to discover that they were all but gone. They'd been superficial at the most. The biggest blow had been to his dignity.

"Don't worry. He'll be gone tomorrow, and then things can get back to normal."

With a final caress she left him to his fitful nap.

In Sew Welcome's craft room she found Sadie and Mary Ann hard at work on the quilt's binding, the last step before calling the project complete. Betty perched on a nearby chair with Frank resting peacefully in her lap.

"This quilt is so beautiful," Betty was saying as Liz entered. "It makes me want to take up quilting."

"We offer classes." Mary Ann spoke without looking up from her needlework. "Next time you come, you should arrange a longer stay and take advantage of them. We'd love to have you join us."

Betty stroked her pet. "I might do that."

To Liz, the statement sounded like a threat. If Frank returned, Beans might well run away from home. The next time Betty called to reserve a room, she would specify the rules right up front—Devious Frank must be supervised at all times or left at home.

Liz got her sewing box from its place on the shelves, noting the plethora of items stored there. "We're going to have quite a chore painting this room."

"I think we should hire someone," Sadie said. "Can't imagine it would cost much."

Mary Ann looked up to examine the shelves. "It'll be more than you think. The shelving will need to be painted as well, not just the walls. We have a lot of shelves."

Betty spoke up. "My brother would do it, and he wouldn't charge much."

"Really?" Liz tried to imagine the surly Benjamin performing the work at a discount, and failed.

"I'm positive." She lowered her voice, worry plain in her expression. "He's fallen on hard times, the poor dear. Why, just last night he had to borrow money from me to tide him over until he finds another job."

In her usual blunt manner, Sadie asked, "If he's so hard up what's he doing here on vacation? The rent on those cabins isn't cheap."

The same question had occurred to Liz.

Betty bristled. "He desperately needed a break. That place where he worked was beastly. They took shameful advantage of his sweet nature and nearly worked him to death."

If Benjamin possessed a sweet nature, he'd kept it hidden last night. Of course, Betty thought Cranky Cat was an angel too.

Sadie worked another stitch. "I've got a bathroom that needs painting. Maybe I could hire him to do that, and we can see what his work is like. Do you think he would be up for it?"

Betty gave her a pleased look. "I'll ask him."

The image of the paint pyramid hovered in Liz's mind. "If you don't mind beige, you can have a gallon of the stuff I bought at the auction. I've decided against painting my quarters for the time being, and I'm sure the rest will be more than enough for this room."

Sadie nodded. "Thanks. I'll take it. But I can't imagine when we'll have time to dismantle all these shelves, right in the middle of tourist season."

Liz laughed. "I thought the same thing. Maybe we could just do the workroom for now."

"Good idea."

"I've been meaning to ask what you've done with your purchases." Mary Ann tied off a stitch and snipped the thread.

"I put the lamps in the third-floor guest rooms and the DVDs in the library." She rolled her eyes. "The napkin rings are in the junk drawer in the kitchen."

"What about the trunk?"

"I'm having buyer's remorse about that. I really don't have any place for it. I've considered selling it to Gavin."

"Oh, I'd rethink that," Mary Ann said.

After learning the extent of his behavior toward Leah Schwartz, and especially after catching him outside the Sunset Room, Liz was inclined to agree.

"If you're serious about not wanting it, I'll buy it from you." Sadie's needle stabbed at the fabric. "If nothing more than to keep him from getting it."

"You know what?" Liz smiled at her. "It's yours. Consider it a gift."

Her reward was one of those trademark smiles that seemed to take possession of Sadie's entire face.

They worked in a companionable silence for a while, the three of them making good progress on the binding, while Betty observed. Liz anticipated the afternoon's visit with pleasure. Would Dinah let them hold her brand-new son?

A noise from the shop entrance alerted them to someone's arrival. "Surprise, surprise!"

Liz looked up to see the last person she expected. "Kiera!" She anchored her needle and hurried over to wrap the young woman in a hug. "Why aren't you at college?"

The embrace held the warmth of friendship, and Liz almost didn't want to release her.

"I came for the homecoming game last night." She made the rounds of the table, bestowing a hug on Mary Ann and Sadie. When she got to Betty, she stopped. "Oh, hello. What a pretty kitty."

Frank arched his back under her caress, while Betty preened. *Pretty is as pretty does*, Liz's mother used to say.

"Goodness, look at you." Sadie made a show of sweeping the girl from head to toe. "College life agrees with you. You've put on some weight."

Mary Ann added, "You look fit."

"Can't imagine how I've gained a pound, since I spend my days running from one end of campus to the other, and I've only been there a few weeks." She grinned. "The food at the Commons is pretty good though." Then she turned an inquisitive look on Liz. "Hey, what's wrong with Beans?"

With an effort, Liz did not allow her gaze to flicker toward Frank. "What do you mean?"

"I thought he'd be all over me, but he hardly moved when I came in. He seems kind of . . ." She searched for a word. "Droopy."

Sadie barked a laugh. "More than usual, you mean?"

"Actually, yeah. Like he's depressed or something."

"He's had a few challenges to deal with lately," Liz said. "He'll be fine in a day or two."

Kiera nodded and then examined the quilt. "Hey, look at this one. That's really nice. Is it for anyone special?"

They spent a moment discussing Dinah's baby. The conversation expanded to include updates on the people around Pleasant Creek. Liz stood back and watched the young woman. What a change from the dour girl who had showed up when Liz first bought the inn and practically insisted that Liz hire her. She'd always been bright, but now intelligence shone in her clear green eyes, and her easy manner spoke of a sense of well-being that Liz had prayed the girl would achieve. It took a strong person to rise from such humble beginnings, and Liz could not have been prouder if Kiera was her own daughter.

When the conversation lagged, Liz looped an arm through Kiera's. "While you're here, could I get you to help me with something?"

She grinned. "I just got here and already you're putting me to work?"

Liz laughed. "Something like that. I need some help moving a few things and figured I could make use of your strong young back."

"Sure thing. What have you got?"

Liz led her through the house and into her private quarters. "I need help loading that trunk and a gallon of paint in Sadie's car." A thought halted her. "I hope she didn't ride her motorcycle today."

"She didn't. I saw her Jeep in the driveway."

While Kiera tested the weight of the trunk, Liz went to her desk and slid open the middle drawer, where she kept a bit of cash. She extracted two twenties and then turned to offer them to the girl.

Kiera raised her hands. "You don't have to pay me to help you move a couple of things."

"This isn't a payment." Liz tucked the money into the pocket of the girl's jeans. "It's a gift. I missed your birthday, and I know college students are always short on cash. Just take it."

The hands came down and then wrapped around Liz in a quick hug that warmed her heart. "Thanks. You're awesome, you know that?"

"So are you." Then she gestured toward the trunk. "While we're at it, you can help me take the rest of the paint to Sew Welcome. Every time I look at it I feel guilty, like I should be doing something with it."

They accomplished the tasks in short order. The trunk didn't quite fit in the back of Sadie's Jeep, so they set it and a can of paint in the back seat. The other paint cans they lined up along the rear wall of Sew Welcome's craft room. Mary Ann said she'd make room in the storage closet when they finished the binding on the baby quilt.

The chore accomplished, Kiera said, "Is Sarah upstairs? I want to say hi."

"I think she's just finishing up in the Heirloom Room."

Liz waved toward the staircase, and then smiled after the young woman as she left. The friendship between Sarah and Kiera was another thing to be thankful for. At first theirs had been a stormy relationship, and the conflict between her two young employees had weighed heavily on Liz. Thankfully, all the misunderstandings had been cleared up, and they got along famously now.

Betty stood, clutching Frank to her chest. "I believe I'll take a drive out to Benjamin's cabin and mention that painting job."

Liz started to remind her to either take her cat with her or close him in the bedroom, but she hated to badger the woman. Instead, she picked up her needle to resume her work on the quilt. Before she could take the first stitch the inn's doorbell rang.

Mary Ann raised her head and looked toward the shop entrance. "You aren't expecting any other guests, are you?"

Only visitors to the inn rang the bell. The locals knew they were welcome to come inside during the day, when the door was unlocked.

"No. I'm at the bursting point now."

Liz left her needle in the unbound edge of the fabric and headed out the shop door.

On the front porch she found two men dressed in conservative Amish clothing. One was known to her—tall and thin, his white beard in sharp contrast to his black coat. The other was not familiar.

"Bishop Manz." Liz looked into the hard eyes belonging to the older man. "This is a . . . pleasant surprise." Perhaps she would be forgiven the fib. She had not had many dealings with the bishop, but when she did she found him a fair man, though somewhat reticent and occasionally hard. Not the kind of man one would invite for a friendly chat over coffee.

"I would like to speak with you about a matter of importance." He spoke without smiling, his words heavily accented with the local Bernese Swiss dialect native to the Amish of Pleasant Creek.

A list of possible transgressions she might have committed flitted through Liz's mind, though she had no reason to feel that way. The bishop's stern countenance reminded her of her principal in elementary school and reduced her to a ten-year-old caught snitching an extra treat from the teacher's candy jar.

Gulping back the ridiculous feelings, she swung the door open. "Certainly. Please come in."

As the other man entered, she offered a smile. "I don't believe we've met. I'm Liz Eckardt."

He ducked his head, which was covered with a round-brimmed hat. "Asa Schwartz."

Leah Schwartz's father. There could only be one reason for a visit from these two men.

She led them to the sitting room and indicated that they should be seated. They each selected cushionless hard-backed chairs and perched on the edge in identical poses, knees and heels together.

"May I get you something to drink and a slice of cinnamon cake?"

"Dänka, but *nay*," the bishop said. "We will not take much of your time."

Liz seated herself on the sofa across from him, her hands folded in her lap. The reason for the visit must be serious, indeed. The Amish placed a high value on hospitality and would stop whatever they were doing when visitors came to call. To refuse the offer of food spoke volumes about the nature of this visit.

Bishop Manz glanced at Asa. "We have heard news that disturbs us greatly. I hope it is not true."

"Tell me what you've heard."

"That you have a man staying here who has caused much pain to my community."

As she had suspected, this visit was about Gavin. She should have known it the moment she saw the bishop on the porch. "You're referring to Gavin Younger."

At the mention of Gavin's name, Asa's features hardened until they seemed to be carved from stone. Liz shifted on the cushion, uncomfortable with the waves of disapproval directed toward her.

The bishop winced, as though hearing the name hurt him. "That is the one."

Liz clenched her hands together. Just last night she had refused to confirm Gavin's presence to a gruff voice on the phone. This, however, was different. Bishop Manz was highly respected not only by his Amish flock but by everyone in Pleasant Creek. She knew him.

"That is true. He is a guest here."

"We had hoped to discover the information false." The bishop leaned toward her, holding her gaze with his. "This man has done irreparable damage to many people."

Liz glanced at Asa before replying. "I know about Leah."

Asa stiffened. "And still you invited him to stay here?" Though he spoke quietly, outrage made his voice intensely uncomfortable.

Though Liz was under no obligation to explain her actions to anyone, her heart went out to this man. What father wouldn't be devastated at losing his daughter? And she respected the stern-faced bishop. During her time in Pleasant Creek he had demonstrated that he took his responsibilities seriously and truly cared about those he led. Her first encounter with Bishop Manz had been contentious when she informed him of her suspicions regarding the illegal activity of one of his Amish congregants. When she was proven right, he had responded with dignity and even gratitude. She'd fought hard to gain his respect and would like to keep it.

She directed her answer to him. "I learned the details only this morning. I can assure you that if I had known them before he arrived, I would not have allowed him to stay."

"But you know now."

The statement held a request, the same one Sarah had voiced earlier. "He's already paid for lodging until tomorrow."

"Miss Eckardt, I have been given a responsibility by *Gött* to guide the people in this district. I am to provide for them and teach them to love Him and love each other according to our ways. That provision is not merely to ensure each family has enough to eat and clothing to wear." Again he leaned forward and fixed her with a direct stare. "My greatest role is to guide their eternal souls. This man you are sheltering led one of my precious charges astray."

Now it was Asa's turn to wince, though he did not unclench his fists.

Liz held the bishop's gaze without blinking. "I understand that, and believe me, I sympathize. But unless he does something illegal or causes a problem with another guest, I'm afraid I can't ask him to leave."

The memory of finding him outside the Sunset Room returned. If she had discovered him *inside* the room, that would have justified an eviction. But she hadn't.

A struggle played across the bishop's face. Several times his lips parted, as if he was going to speak, but then shut. Liz watched him. He had something else to say, but wasn't sure he should.

"What is it, sir?"

"This man is dishonest. I know it here." He pressed a fist to his chest. "You would do well to take care while he is under your roof."

The words struck at Liz. She had no doubt the bishop was entirely accurate in his estimation of Gavin's character. But was there even more to worry about? In addition to being dishonest, was he also dangerous?

No. I've already ruled out him killing his aunt. He had no reason to—and plenty of reasons not *to.*

And yet the murder of Louise Younger remained unsolved.

The hair on her arms prickled.

"I will," she promised. She sent an unspoken apology toward Asa. "And it's only for one more night."

Bishop Manz stood and settled his round-brimmed hat more firmly on his head. Asa followed suit.

"Tomorrow cannot come too soon," the bishop said.

Since tomorrow she would see the last of both Gavin and Betty's sneaky cat, Liz couldn't agree more. "Amen to that."

9

Liz stood on the front porch, watching until Bishop Manz's buggy turned the corner and passed out of view. Still she stayed, listening to the receding *clip-clop* of his horse's hooves. Their conversation played itself over and over in her mind, and she couldn't shake the sense of foreboding that Gavin would find some way to make trouble before his departure from Pleasant Creek. *Well, more trouble than he has simply by being here.*

The day's weather continued the pattern of the week's unseasonable warmth. The sun shone with dazzling beauty in a gloriously clear sky. A desire to see bright rays sparkle on the surface of the lake overtook her, and she descended the steps. The Olde Mansion Inn loomed above her, and she paused a moment to gaze at the charming red-brick structure with its clean white trim. The sight helped to soothe the uneasy feelings the bishop's visit had stirred up. When she had left her legal practice and bought this place, she'd had so many doubts. What was a lawyer doing trying to run a B&B? She'd come searching for answers to the mysteries of her mother's past and had found the path to her own happy future.

Rounding the corner of the house, she stooped to pull a stray weed from the neat flower bed. The yellow and orange mums still bloomed, but soon it would be time to cut them back to the ground level and prepare the garden for winter.

Laughter rang in the clear, fresh air. Liz recognized the voice as Kiera's and indulged in a smile. She and Sarah had apparently picked up their friendship right where they left off. She quickened her step toward the backyard, eager to see the two together.

When she spied Kiera, Liz came to an abrupt halt. She wasn't laughing with Sarah at all. Standing beside her beneath the gazebo was Gavin. He leaned casually against one of the posts and looked down at Keira, who stood close, her face tilted up to his. He said something, and the young woman laughed.

Worry tied tight knots in Liz's stomach as she covered the distance between them at something just short of a trot.

"Hello." She forced a smile for Kiera. "I didn't realize you were still here." She switched her gaze to Gavin. "Or you either. I thought you'd gone out."

"I came back." He gave Kiera a look of unconcealed admiration. "And boy, am I glad I did."

Alarm bells rang in Liz's mind. "Uh, Kiera, I wonder if I might have a word with you." She hardened her gaze and turned it on Gavin. "Alone."

"Sure." Gavin straightened. "I'm going to meet some friends for lunch soon anyway." He looked down at Kiera again, displaying a lopsided grin. "I'll see you around seven?"

Heat flared under Liz's collar when the girl nodded, beaming. They had a date tonight? With a glance in her direction, Gavin sauntered off. They watched until he disappeared around the edge of the inn.

"So, what did you want to talk about?"

Words failed Liz. How should she approach this conversation? Kiera had come a long way from the prickly girl who first showed up at the bed-and-breakfast, but she was still a strong-minded young woman who might not be open to unsolicited advice about her romantic pursuits.

"Why don't we sit down?" Liz gestured to the bench, and with a shrug, Kiera dropped onto it. "How do you know Gavin?"

"He was a few years ahead of me in high school." She shrugged. "We met up last night at the homecoming game. He used to get in trouble a lot, but now he seems like a nice guy." An un-Kiera-like girlish giggle escaped her lips. "And he's always been cute."

"Sometimes looks can be deceiving."

The girl's eyes narrowed. "What do you mean by that?"

Out with it, Liz.

"I don't want you to think I'm meddling, but I wish you'd steer clear of that young man."

"Why?" Thankfully, she sounded more curious than offended.

Liz bit down on her lip. How much should she share? She didn't hold with gossip, especially malicious gossip that consisted more of suspicion than proven fact. On the other hand, she felt protective of Kiera.

Stick with the facts.

"His aunt was recently murdered."

Compassion flooded the girl's features. "I know. He told me. Isn't that sad? His mom threw him out when he was a teenager, and his aunt was the only person who would take him in."

"It *is* sad, but before she died she cut him out of her will, so obviously their relationship wasn't good."

Kiera leaned forward. "But don't you see? That makes it even sadder. Now he'll never be able to make up with her."

"True." Liz dared not voice Sadie's opinion of Gavin's role in his aunt's death, not without a shred of proof. Time for another approach. "When Gavin lived here, apparently he got into a lot of trouble. He had a reputation for being something of a delinquent."

"I know." Chuckling, she shook her head. "Knocking over mailboxes and toilet-papering people's houses."

"He did far worse than that."

"What do you mean?"

Liz explained what she'd learned about Leah Schwartz. She also confided a bit about the bishop's visit, and the strength of Sarah's disapproval.

As she talked, understanding crept over Kiera's face. "I see where this is going. You're afraid he'll do the same to me. Corrupt me or something." She grasped Liz's hands in hers. "How sweet for you to be concerned. But really, Liz, you don't need to worry. I can take care of myself."

"I'm sure you can." Though she wasn't sure at all. "But I'd hate to see you hurt."

"It's not even a date, not really. We're just going to grab a burger and talk." She squeezed Liz's hand. "I can handle myself. It'll be okay, Liz."

There was no use arguing. Liz could see that her mind was made up. She forced a smile. "Would you do me a favor anyway? Ask Sarah what she thinks of him before you go." Maybe someone closer to her own age could convince her.

"If it will make you feel better, fine." Kiera released her hand and stood. "I'll talk to Sarah. But I promise you, there's nothing to worry about."

She headed in the direction of the house, leaving Liz alone to stare out over Jaynes Lake. The dazzling sun overhead failed to lighten the worry that darkened her thoughts. She did not doubt for one minute that Gavin was as much of a troublemaker today as when he had lived in Pleasant Creek. Too many disturbing things had happened since his arrival, like the menacing phone call and his "confusion" over the third-floor guest rooms. But did he pose a physical threat to Kiera? She had no reason to think so.

And yet . . .

"Yeah, I heard he was back in town. Haven't run into him yet, though. He's probably going out of his way to stay out of mine."

Stan Houghton, Pleasant Creek's shrewd police chief, chuckled at his own joke. Liz pressed the phone to her ear and settled on the comfy love seat in her small living room.

"I wish he felt the same about me." She kicked off her shoes and curled her feet beneath her. "He's done nothing but ruffle feathers since he arrived."

"That business with the Schwartz girl?"

So Stan knew about Leah Schwartz. No surprise there. He made it his business to know everything that involved the residents of Pleasant Creek.

"That's a big part of it. But I'm more concerned about his recent activities. You heard his aunt was murdered in Fort Wayne."

The casual tone changed. Now she had the attention of Police Chief Houghton. "I heard. Do you have reason to suspect he was involved?"

"No," Liz hurried to say. "Nothing concrete. But we ran into him at her estate auction, and he acted suspiciously. Then he showed up here that night, and he's received a phone call from an extremely unfriendly mystery man. Now he's taking Kiera Williams out on a date." When she spelled it out like that, her misgivings sounded silly.

"She's of legal age, isn't she?"

"Yes, but—"

"Liz, what is it you want me to do? I can't arrest a man for asking a girl out."

Despite feeling slightly foolish, Liz plowed ahead. "Couldn't you just check his record and see if he has any recent criminal activity? You must know someone in the Fort Wayne police department. If they're investigating Gavin as a suspect in Louise's death they'd tell you, wouldn't they?"

"Probably, but I couldn't tell you."

She nodded. Lawyer Liz knew the prohibitions against discussing an ongoing investigation with outsiders. But she still had to try. "If I have a suspected murderer staying under my roof I have a right to know."

"The key word is *suspected.* Any inside information I get would be confidential." A pause, and then he continued in a placating tone. "I'll make a couple of calls. But if you're really concerned then why did you rent a room to him?"

"I felt sorry for him. And another guest put me in an awkward position in front of him." She sighed. "Honestly, I don't think he killed his aunt. My mind keeps circling back to that because of a comment Sadie made."

Now he laughed. "You know I have a world of respect for Sadie Schwarzentruber, but you can't convict the guy based on a comment by a woman whose mailbox he blew up with firecrackers when he was a kid."

"I didn't know that." That would explain Sadie's intense dislike of Gavin, though.

"We never proved he did it, just like a lot of his stunts. But she believes it, and she's probably right."

"To be honest, I'm being an overprotective mother hen." The confession felt good, and she relaxed again against the cushion. "I love Kiera, and I don't want to see her get involved with an unsavory person."

"Neither do I. Like I said, I'll make a few calls. If I come up with any reason for concern, I promise I'll be all over him."

"Thanks, Stan. I appreciate it."

She ended the call and then headed toward Sew Welcome. Time to finish that quilt.

Work on the quilt had progressed to the point that Liz felt like a useless appendage. Mary Ann and Sadie were down to the binding on the last side, which made it difficult for three people to work at the same time. Instead, Liz perched on a stool and watched. She hadn't been there long when a familiar figure entered the room.

"Jackson!" She smiled a greeting for the Pleasant Creek mayor and owner of Cross Furniture Company. "What are you doing here in the middle of the day?"

The skin at the corners of his eyes crinkled when he returned her smile. "I got a chocolate craving." He held up a white paper bag. "Sweet Everything has the best brownies in the state."

"Naomi's brownies are good," Sadie agreed, "but nothing satisfies a yearning for chocolate like Mary Ann's mudslide pie."

Hope sprang into the handsome face. "Do you have one?"

"Sadly, no." Mary Ann grinned. "But if you could arrange to have another craving tomorrow, I might be able to accommodate you."

"I already feel it coming on."

He opened the bag and offered it to the quilting pair, but both ladies declined. Moving with an easy grace reminiscent of an athlete, he approached Liz. When the bag came within sniffing range, the aroma of chocolate tantalized her nose. She caved. The fudgy treat still held a trace of warmth, and she relished every delicious morsel.

Jackson bit into a brownie and chewed with obvious enjoyment. When he'd finished, he leaned against the counter, his long legs stretched out before him.

"Actually, I wanted to come see you anyway."

Liz ignored a rush of warmth and the quick, knowing looks tossed her way by her friends. "Oh?"

"The guys over at the shop are up in arms about one of your guests. They've talked about nothing else all day."

"Gee, I wonder who that is." Sarcasm lay heavy in Sadie's comment.

"If you're referring to Gavin, then yes. He is staying here." When Jackson opened his mouth, Liz hurried on. "But only for one more day. Tomorrow he'll go back home to Kentucky and everyone can breathe a sigh of relief. Including me."

"Well, if any graffiti shows up on the clock tower before he leaves town, I'll know where to send the police," Jackson said. He grew solemn. "Seriously, stay on your toes while he's here."

Her worries over Kiera returned. "Why do you say that? He's obviously led a checkered past, but I don't think he's violent or anything." She watched Jackson closely. "Do you?"

He answered with a shrug. "I don't know what he's into these days. All I know is he's caused a lot of heartache for a lot of people around here." He caught and held her gaze. "Just be careful. I wouldn't want anything to happen to any of your guests. Or you."

Battling emotions erupted, and Liz's insides twisted into knots. Jackson's concern for her was touching, but did he consider her a helpless female, unable to take care of herself and her business?

In the next instant the irony of the thought struck her, and she almost laughed. That was exactly how she'd just treated Kiera.

"I'll be careful," she promised, smiling. "And thanks. I wouldn't want anything to happen to me either."

10

Shortly after Jackson left, Mary Ann clipped the final thread on the Churn Dash baby quilt.

"There." She stuck her needle into a pincushion and the three of them stood back to admire their handiwork.

"It is absolutely precious," Liz announced. "Dinah will be thrilled with it."

"I think she'll be pleased." Mary Ann ran a hand over the surface. "I'm glad we prewashed the fabric, since we don't have time before we deliver it."

"She'll probably wash the quilt before she uses it anyway," Sadie said. "I would."

Liz glanced at her watch. Just past twelve thirty. "When do you want to head out there? I need to be back in time to bake cookies for coffee hour."

"Oh, we won't stay that long." A silver lock of hair waved above Mary Ann's eyebrow, and she absently brushed it away. "Tell you what. Why don't we go now? We can grab a bite to eat on the way."

An impromptu lunch with her friends? Though the brownie had nearly filled her up, Liz wouldn't miss such a rare opportunity. "Perfect. Let me go take Beans out for a minute and then I'll grab my purse and a jacket."

She headed out and ran smack into someone coming in.

"Oh, sorry." Gavin steadied her with a hand on each shoulder. "Didn't mean to crash into you. You okay?"

"I'm fine." She stepped backward and peered at him. "I thought you were meeting friends for lunch."

"I am. I had to make a call first." He tossed a smile over her shoulder. "Hello ladies. Hard at work on another blanket I see."

"It's a *quilt*." The acid in Sadie's tone could have burned through steel.

"Whatever." He flipped a hand in the air. "I just popped in to ask what time checkout is tomorrow."

"Eleven," Liz answered automatically. "Unless you go to church, and then I'll extend it until one."

His features scrunched in a scowl. "Eleven it is."

He started to turn away, but then halted. His face went white as his eyes fixed on something behind her. Liz half-turned to glance in that direction, but saw nothing that would elicit such a reaction. Sadie was folding the quilt, and Mary Ann stood at the ribbon shelves. The counter contained the usual assortment of items, and in front of it—

Ah. Four gallons of paint sat in a row on the floor in front of the counter. The paint she'd bought at Louise's auction, and that Gavin said he had purchased for his aunt. A visual reminder of his recent loss. Once again her feelings about the young man wavered, and her heart went out to Louise's grieving nephew.

She turned back to him and asked softly, "Are you okay?"

"Uh—" His mouth snapped shut. "Yeah. Of course."

The corners of his lips twitched upward in a smile that failed to reach his eyes, and then he left.

Acting on impulse, Liz followed him into the shop's small entryway and stopped him with a hand on the arm. "Gavin, could I talk to you about Kiera?"

The nonchalance he adopted looked entirely put on. "What about her?"

"I know she looks like a strong young woman but she *is* still young."

"Plenty old enough to look after herself." The meaning he poured into the words was perfectly clear. He wanted Liz to mind her own business.

She gritted her teeth. "I know that, but I care about her. She's worked for me since I bought this place, so I feel responsible for her."

A shrewd looked dawned on his features, and he folded his arms across his chest. "What are you getting at? Are you asking me to cancel our date tonight?"

Though that was exactly what she'd hoped to accomplish with this conversation, Liz hesitated. Kiera would be furious with her for interfering.

Before she could formulate an answer, he shook his head. "Look, I'm not as bad as everybody in this town seems to think I am. Sure, I pulled a few pranks when I lived here. So what? I was a kid. And yeah, I dated an Amish girl." His gaze sharpened. "Who was legally an adult, I should add. It's not like I killed anybody or anything."

At the last sentence, a chill raced up Liz's spine. Was that guilt speaking? "Why would you say that?"

His fingers raked through his hair, a habit she'd noticed he indulged in when nervous. Or maybe angry?

"Look, I know the way the people in this town think. They're probably all saying I killed Aunt Louise." A hard set came over his jaw. "That ticks me off. The police over in Fort Wayne apparently thought the same thing. They called the cops down in Kentucky, and I got a visit from the local yokels back home."

A deep flush stained his face. Liz struggled to keep her expression calm. "The police questioned you about your aunt's death?"

"Yeah, isn't that just great? I didn't even know she'd died until they showed up with a ton of questions." He dropped his arms to his sides, hands clenched into fists. "Do me a favor, would you? Tell all those small-town and small-minded gossips that I have an airtight alibi."

He aimed a glare behind her, apparently convinced that Sadie and Mary Ann were fueling the gossip. Liz would have questioned him further about the nature of his alibi, but he stormed away. A few seconds later the front door slammed behind him.

Mary Ann's calm voice broke the tension. "Well, that was unpleasant."

She turned to find her friends watching from inside the craft room. Liz sagged against the door frame. "You're telling me."

Sadie scowled after him. "He was a little too vehement in his denial if you ask me."

"That reaction *could* be from grief." Liz hated to discount the depth of emotion anyone would feel at the loss of a loved one. Especially a young man who was now without the only relative he felt cared about him. An image of Steve rose in her mind's eye, along with a sharp pang of sorrow. Oh, how she missed him.

Selecting a roll of ribbon from the shelf, Mary Ann picked up a pair of scissors on her way back to the table. "Let's not talk about Gavin anymore. Where would you girls like to go to lunch?"

Liz welcomed the change of subject. She'd prefer not to *think* about Gavin anymore, either. The feelings he stirred in her were too close to home. "I'm fine with whatever you decide," she told them on her way out. "I'll meet you outside."

Beans lay in his usual spot in the foyer, his eyes open and fixed on the doorway leading into the rotunda. Liz followed his gaze. He enjoyed a perfect view of the bottom of the stairway.

"Don't worry," she told the mournful dog. "Betty told me she was going to put Crazy Kitty in her room before she left. He won't bother you."

Brown eyes flickered toward her, but apparently he wasn't reassured. He returned to his vigil.

"Come on. Up and at 'em." She bent over and hauled him to his feet by the collar. "I'm leaving for a little while, so you need to go outside for a minute."

The fact that he followed her through the front door with only the slightest of protests spoke to the depth of his depression. He walked with his ears drooping and his stub of a tail tucked even tighter than usual. Liz was tempted to leave him outside to soak up some vitamin D, but she didn't have the heart. In this mood he'd probably just sit by the door the whole time, waiting for someone to let him in.

She squatted down in front of him and lifted his head in both of her hands. "Listen, Beans. There's something you don't understand. You're a dog. Frank is a cat. Cats are supposed to be afraid of dogs, not the other way around."

He drooped further, as though he understood perfectly and was ashamed of his inability to stand up to his canine reputation. With an affectionate rub of her pet's jowls, she stood. At least he trotted after her when she descended the porch stairs and stepped into the grass. She decided to take the long way around and enter the house through the four-season room. That way he'd get a few steps of exercise.

She kept her pace slow so Beans could sniff every shrub and flower. When she reached the back of the inn she heard a familiar voice and headed toward the driveway. Sure enough, Gavin and Mary Ann stood beside her car. Gavin's arms were folded tightly across his chest, and his face displayed a defensive expression that bordered on insolence. Liz picked up her pace.

"I don't think you fully realize the impact that Leah's leaving had on her community." Mary Ann's tone remained even, though there was no mistaking the hint of sorrow. "They blame you for luring her away from her home, her family. Her faith."

"I did not *lure* her away, and I'm sick of being blamed." Gavin raked his fingers through his curly hair. "She was looking for an excuse to leave anyway."

Liz arrived at their side. Sadie was already seated in the car, but watched the encounter through the windshield with sharp eyes.

Mary Ann drew in a breath. “I think you’d have a hard time convincing her parents and friends of that.”

A sullen pout tugged at Gavin’s lips. “I don’t have to convince anyone. Let them ask her, if they really want to know. Leah was fed up with her life on the farm and her father acting like a dictator about what she could do and who she could see. If I hadn’t come along, she would have run away on her own eventually.”

Doubt colored Mary Ann’s kind features. “I’ve known her since she was born, and I recognized a touch of restlessness in her. But without a catalyst of some sort, she would have settled down eventually.”

“Yeah?” He planted a hand on his hip. “So then why didn’t she come home when we broke up? Her family would have taken her back. Heck, I offered to drive her up here. If she was such a good Amish girl, why isn’t she here instead of living in a dump in Indianapolis?”

Mary Ann shook her head. “I understand you feel unjustly accused, but her family will never believe she would leave on her own.”

Again, his arms folded and he scowled. “They can believe what they want. It’s no skin off my nose. But I was there the last time her family visited our apartment. She threw them out and told them never to come back.”

He stomped off toward the back of the house before Mary Ann could reply. But before he rounded the corner, he turned back toward them and addressed Liz.

“As for that Kiera chick, I know you guys think she’s too good for the likes of me.”

Liz couldn’t help feeling a little sorry for him. What must it be like to have everyone believe the worst? Even though it might be true.

“I’m sorry if you’ve gotten that impression. As I said before, Kiera is like family to us. We care about her and don’t want her to be hurt.”

Shaking his head, he snorted. "Well you can stop worrying about her. She's old enough to make her own decisions, just like Leah was. But if it makes you feel better, I have no plans to steal her away or corrupt her, or whatever it is you seem to think I'm going to do. I'm not even picking her up. We're going to meet at the restaurant and have a hamburger. Period. End of story."

When he had stomped out of sight and out of earshot, Liz released a breath she hadn't known she was holding and turned to Mary Ann. "Do you think there's any truth to what he said, that Leah doesn't want to come home?"

Mary Ann nodded sadly. "I'm afraid he might be right. Viola told me herself. Leah said she would never return, and she hasn't. Viola cried for months."

"I'm so sorry." The words seemed inadequate in the face of a mother's longing for her child's return. Liz knew something about that herself, with Steve away in Kosovo. But his absence was entirely different. How devastating it must be to suffer a beloved child's rejection.

Sadie rolled down the window. "That young man has a lot of anger. I still wish Kiera wouldn't go out with him."

Actually, Gavin's parting tirade had gone a long way toward calming Liz's fears about his date with Kiera. He sounded completely sincere. They would share a burger and probably catch up on news about some of the people they both knew.

"I think she'll be fine." She poured confidence into her smile. "I don't know about you, but I feel better knowing they're meeting at the restaurant instead of riding together."

Mary Ann nodded. "I do too."

Beans slumped around the corner and dragged himself toward them. He slouched up to Liz and turned his head to cast a mournful look in the direction of the house.

"Oh, all right," she told the dog. "You've had a bit of sunshine." To Mary Ann and Sadie she said, "I'll put him inside and grab my purse. Be right back."

She opened the back door for Beans and followed him into the house. He crossed the four-season room in the direction of the kitchen, but when he reached the entrance he stopped dead in the doorframe. A pathetic whimper sounded from his smooshed-up nostrils.

"What's wrong now?" She shook her head and stepped around him. "I thought you'd get used to that raised feeding tray by n—"

The sight in the corner of the kitchen explained Beans's whine. Lounging on the feeding tray like a sphinx was Frank. His black-and-white body draped from one side of the shelf to the other in the narrow space behind the food and water bowls. Ignoring Liz completely, he fixed his amber stare on Beans, the tip of his tail flicking the air. That the cat had chosen the location purposefully was obvious. He was taunting Beans.

"What are you doing in here?" Liz crossed the room and picked up the cat. He lay limply in her arms and meowed meekly. "You're supposed to be in your room."

Beans left his post in the doorway, slumped across the floor, and sniffed at his food bowl. Then without taking a bite, he slunk from the room in the direction of the foyer.

Holding the cat firmly, Liz marched up the stairs to the Amish Room. The door stood open a few inches, just wide enough for the fugitive feline to slip through.

Liz set him on the carpet. "Now stay there."

She pulled the door shut and locked it behind her. What was it with this batch of guests that they didn't see the need to lock their rooms?

11

Liz gazed down into the tiny face of Dinah's newborn. "He is amazing," she whispered.

They sat in the Stoltzfus living room, where Dinah and her husband lived. As often happened in the Amish community, the newly married couple had moved into the family home, where Seth continued to help his father with the farm. As the youngest son, he would one day take over running the family business, and Dinah the management of the household, while the retired parents moved next door into the smaller *Grossdawdy Haus*. For now, they shared the home with Seth's parents and his two younger sisters, both of whom hovered over the baby with beaming smiles.

Dinah sat on a straight-backed wooden chair beside Liz. Though Amish eschewed the luxury of upholstery, a concession had been made for the new mother in the form of a pillow, which she used as a cushion.

"*Ja*, he is." Dinah's face glowed with love.

Perfect little lips pursed and moved in a sucking motion. It was impossible to tell whom the infant resembled, since his face was still puffy from birth, but Liz fancied she glimpsed a touch of his grandfather in the tiny features. Amos Miller was Dinah's father and Liz's uncle, her deceased mother's older brother. Wonder stole over Liz as she again realized that this baby was part of her own family, a family she had not known until she moved to Pleasant Creek.

Standing behind the rocking chair where Liz sat with the baby, Mary Ann peered over her shoulder. "What have you decided to name him?"

"He is Joshua, after Seth's *Grossvater*."

"Joshua." A good Biblical name, of which the Amish were fond. The sleeping infant stirred, and Liz rocked in the chair, snuggling the warm bundle close as she'd done when Steve was a baby. Though he had not come to live with her until he was seven years old, his mother had been a dear friend, and Liz had never missed an opportunity to visit her godson. "Hush, little Joshua," she uttered in a quiet, singsong voice. "Go back to sleep."

"Dänka for the beautiful quilt." Dinah ran a hand over their gift, folded and tied with blue ribbon. "Such perfect stitches. I could never make something this detailed."

Mary Ann dismissed the comment. "Of course you could. When you're feeling up to it, you should join us for a quilting class. You can bring the baby with you."

"Okay, your time is up. You can't hog him for the whole visit." Sadie left her chair and came to stand in front of Liz, her arms outstretched. "Hand him over."

With a great deal of reluctance, Liz did. Her arms felt empty, bereft. She slid onto a chair across the room and watched Sadie coo at the baby. A wave of longing washed over her, surprising in its strength. How she missed Steve! It had been a long time since she last saw him, and she had no idea when he'd be able to come home again. That was life as a military mom. She knew it, but she didn't have to like it.

He'd certainly been on her mind a lot the past few days. When she got home she'd send him a long, chatty email. Not as good as being able to hug him, but at least she could remind him she loved him.

"I most certainly did!" Betty drew herself up, her considerable chest inflated with outrage. "I shut that door and double-checked it."

Liz pulled on an oven mitt and eyed the woman across the length of the kitchen. "Did you lock it?"

"Of course not." She seemed offended at the thought. "What if a fire broke out? I want the firemen to be able to get in the room quickly to rescue him."

A wave of sweet-scented heat wafted from the oven when Liz opened the door. She waited for the first draft to pass before removing the cookie tray.

"All I can say is, either the door wasn't securely shut, or Frank opened it himself."

Betty sniffed. "Well, he *is* an intelligent cat."

Liz let the comment pass. She highly doubted Frank had figured out how to open a door, intelligent or not. Though he *was* a crafty feline, plus a few additional adjectives she could think of. Nor did she believe Betty had pulled that door closed. An indulgent pet owner, she'd made no secret of the fact that she wanted the cat to have free run of the house, regardless of Liz's request.

Honestly, Liz wouldn't mind having several cats roaming the house. Cats had always appealed to her with their intelligence, independence, and their attention to personal hygiene. But Frank, with his determination to torment Beans, was an entirely different matter.

"I provide locks and keys for your protection as well as my own," she told Betty. "If something valuable disappears, I don't want to be held responsible. I'm sure all my guests are entirely trustworthy, but one can never be too safe."

Though in the matter of Gavin she wasn't *entirely* sure. Even more reason to stress the need to secure Betty's room.

"I'm not naïve enough to travel with valuables. What little jewelry I brought along is secure in my handbag, which goes everywhere with me."

If only the cat went everywhere with her too.

Liz adopted a stern but pleasant tone. "Well, please make sure Frank is *secure* in your room."

The woman gave an offended sniff. "Had I known you were a cat hater, I would have protested when my brother suggested that I procure a room here."

Liz paused in the act of picking up a spatula. "I don't hate cats. I love cats." The time for brutal honesty had arrived. "You may not have noticed, but Frank and Beans don't get along. I'm merely trying to keep the two apart unless they're supervised."

"That's ridiculous. They're the best of friends." Liz might have protested, but Betty continued quickly. "I came down to tell you that I won't be here for coffee hour. My brother and I are driving to Fort Wayne for dinner, and we may take in a movie."

Rarely did the need to confront a guest with anything unpleasant arise, and Liz regretted offending Betty. She was a nice lady and no doubt completely unaware of Frank's psychotic side, which only surfaced in her absence.

"That sounds like a nice evening, but we'll miss visiting with you," she replied with complete sincerity. "For our last night together I made my special white chocolate macadamia nut cookies. Here. Let me give you some to take up to your room."

She slid a pair of hot cookies onto a plate. Looking somewhat appeased, Betty accepted the offering and vacated the kitchen.

It was a small group that gathered in the sitting room for coffee hour that afternoon. The Three Eagles had not yet returned from their day's outing, which Liz hoped meant they were having better luck with the fish than yesterday. Even Caleb did not attend, which put Liz's special cookies in danger of being wasted. Well, not *wasted*, because they'd keep, but they always tasted better fresh.

Otis seemed to agree and helped himself to a third, while his wife ignored the treats, fretful creases heavy on her brow.

"It isn't like Caleb to be so late." She barely took her gaze from the doorway to glance at her husband. "You don't think anything has happened to him, do you?"

"The boy's fine," Otis said around a mouthful of cookie. "Nice weather out there. Great day to soak up some sunshine."

"Where did he go?" Liz asked.

"He said he was going for a walk around the lake, but he should have been back by now."

"Walking all the way around would take a while." Liz selected a pod of hazelnut coffee and slid it into the coffeemaker. "The lake is bigger than it looks from here."

"See, dear?" Otis patted her knee with a patronizing gesture that would have irritated Liz, but which Eunice didn't seem to notice. "Don't be such a worrywart."

Perhaps Eunice was the only helicopter parent.

Beans sat on the cold hearth, a steady and doleful gaze fixed on Liz. Sometimes she could read the dog's mind as easily as if he could speak his requests.

"I'm not lighting a fire tonight," she told him. "The weather has been far too mild today."

She did not add that he shouldn't require the comfort of a fire this evening. After her talk with Betty, she was hopeful that Frank the cat was securely confined in the Amish Room and therefore would not be able to torment the bulldog.

Footsteps in the foyer alerted them to someone's approach, and a moment later Caleb strode into the sitting room. Eunice wasted no time in propelling herself off the sofa and across the floor to gather him in a fierce hug. Then she pushed him back, her hands clutching his arms.

"Where have you been? I've been worried sick."

"I told you, I went for a walk." His tone, though respectful, held a hint of impatience.

"That was hours ago." The whine in Eunice's voice grated across Liz's nerves. "I've called a dozen times, but your cell phone went straight to voice mail."

"The battery died." He shrugged a shoulder. "I forgot to charge it last night."

"This long absence is very inconsiderate of you." The words snapped from Eunice like a cracking whip. "It's not like you to treat your father and me with such disrespect."

"Your mother's right." Otis added a tight-lipped scowl to his stern words. "You owe us an apology."

Spots of color erupted on the teenager's cheeks. His gaze slid toward Liz, who shifted in her seat, embarrassed to witness the public reprimand.

"Sorry," he muttered while staring at his shoes.

"Well." Eunice released her clutch on his arms and smoothed the wrinkles from his sleeves. "You just make sure—"

Thankfully the ringing of the telephone cut into the awkward conversation. Liz had remembered to bring the cordless with her, so she snatched it off the coffee table. "The Olde Mansion Inn, how can I help you?"

"Liz? It's Stan Houghton."

Rising from her chair, Liz told the Porters, "Excuse me while I take this call." Once out of earshot, she spoke into the handset. "Hi Stan. Do you have any news for me?"

"In fact I do. Younger definitely didn't kill his aunt."

Relief wilted Liz's muscles. "I'm glad that's settled. Are you allowed to tell me how you know that?"

"Since it's a matter of public record, yes. At the time Louise Younger was murdered, Gavin was in jail."

The tension returned, and Liz stiffened. "What for?"

"Possession of stolen property. Tried to sell an expensive hot watch to an undercover officer."

"He's a thief?"

Worry for Kiera threatened to plague her, but she dismissed it. Kiera was much smarter than that. No way would she get mixed up with someone who was in trouble with the law. If the young woman had known Gavin had spent time in jail recently on a theft-related charge, she would never have agreed to even a casual meeting over burgers.

"Yep. He couldn't make bond, and his aunt refused, so he sat in jail for three weeks down in Hardin County. The police from Fort Wayne went down there to tell him about his aunt's death and to question him. He had to stay there until his court date, which was Thursday."

The date struck her. "Wait. This past Thursday, as in two days ago?"

"That's right. He would have been in jail longer, but the judge moved his court date up because of his aunt's death."

The day of the auction. No wonder he'd been delayed. Not a traffic jam, as he claimed, but a court appearance, and apparently an early one. So Gavin was a liar and a thief, but at least he wasn't a killer.

"Thanks, Stan. I feel a lot better."

"Thought you would. But keep an eye on your small valuables."

She pressed the disconnect button and returned to the sitting room in time to say goodbye to the Porters.

"We're heading out to grab something to eat," Otis told her. "You're welcome to join us if you don't have plans."

With a broad smile, Liz declined the offer. "Thanks, but you go ahead. I've got some cleaning up to do, and then I plan to enjoy a quiet evening." She stood aside to let them file out of the room. Caleb passed with his head lowered and shoulders slumped, looking very much like Beans since Frank's arrival.

Eunice stopped in the doorway. "Oh, one more thing. Will breakfast be at eight? We're leaving right afterward."

"Gotta hit the road," Otis said. "Long drive ahead of us."

Caleb's head shot up and he drew in a quick breath. Since he stood behind them, his parents didn't notice. Liz avoided looking directly at him, but wondered at the odd reaction. Apparently the time of their departure was news to him, and he wasn't happy about it.

"That's right. Breakfast will be at eight o'clock."

Satisfied, Eunice nodded. "Have a good night."

When Liz had stored the leftover cookies in a zipper bag and cleaned up the dishes, she wandered into her living room. She was kind of hungry, but an inventory of the contents of her refrigerator didn't tempt her appetite. And she'd had a big lunch with Mary Ann and Sadie. A cheeseburger, perhaps? The idea of Kiera's and Gavin's expressions if she entered Burger Heaven during their date made her chuckle. No, definitely not a burger. She'd probably just slap some peanut butter on toast.

She glanced at the clock. Naomi would be closing Sweet Everything soon. On impulse she picked up the phone and dialed her friend's number.

"Hey girl." Naomi's cheerful voice brought a smile to her face. "What's up?"

"You wouldn't happen to have any éclairs left, would you?" Not exactly a healthy dinner option, but an appetizing one. Tomorrow she would eat salad.

"Sure do. Why don't you come over and we'll enjoy a couple together?"

A pleasant visit with her friend over a delicious éclair? Infinitely better than lonely peanut butter toast. Afterward she'd come home, have a nice long soak in a hot bath, and lose herself in that half-finished novel on her bedside table.

"I'll be right there."

The next morning a scratching sound, accompanied by a series of quick yelps, dragged Liz out of a deep sleep. She glanced at the clock on her nightstand. Two thirty a.m. The scratching continued, and she identified the noise as coming from the door that separated her quarters from the inn's kitchen.

"Beans, stop it!" she stage-whispered. "You'll scratch the paint."

What was the matter with him? This wasn't his usual time to go out. Was his tummy upset? Had the poor thing gotten ulcers because of Frank? Tying the belt of her housecoat around her waist, she hurried across her living room and unlocked the door. When she opened it, Beans scurried past her bare feet and ran to the coffee table, which he huddled beneath.

"What in the—?"

A sheet of paper on the floor drew her attention. Someone must have shoved it beneath her door. She picked it up and flipped the light switch so she could read.

Dear Liz,

I know you will be upset when you discover Frank loose in the house. When I arrived home last night and unlocked my door, the poor thing dashed out. I looked for him, but he must have been hiding somewhere, probably huddled beneath a piece of furniture, distressed from having been confined in such a small space for far too long. Probably suffering from claustrophobia. I hope he isn't permanently traumatized. I didn't think you would appreciate me waking the entire house by running through the place calling for him.

Betty

By the time Liz finished the note her teeth were clenched together. *Permanently traumatized? Puh-lease!*

At least that explained Beans's behavior. He'd been terrorized by the ferocious feline again. She dropped to her knees and peered beneath the table.

"What did he do to you? Are you hurt? Come here, boy. It's okay."

She managed to coax him out and look him over. A quick check revealed no new scratches, thank heavens. She retrieved her slippers and a flashlight from the bedroom. Something had sent the dog to her door in search of sanctuary. What had that cat done now?

She shone the beam around as she walked through the house, looking for the gleam of amber eyes. No sign of Frank in the kitchen or the dining room. The door to the utility room was shut, but she peeked inside anyway. Nothing. Nor was he in the rotunda.

The moment she entered the foyer she knew why Beans was so upset. Stretched out on the rug by the door lay the dog's nemesis. Frank had evicted Beans and taken possession of his favorite snoozing place.

The flashlight caught the cat's eyes and turned them into glowing twin circles. He regarded her calmly, the tip of his black-and-white tail swishing back and forth.

"You are a bully." Liz's whisper sounded loud in the quiet house. "You've got your mama fooled, but not me, you sneaky boy."

As she spoke, Liz approached slowly so as not to startle Frank into running away. She knelt and extended her hand while the cat watched, unconcerned. At the first touch of her fingers, he lifted his head and arched his back, inviting the caress to continue down the length of his spine and all the way to the tip of his tail. His mouth opened in a near-silent meow, a clear invitation to repeat the caress. Liz obliged a few times and then picked him up.

"It's time for you to go to bed." She stood, holding the soft, warm body close enough to her chest that she felt the rumble of his purr.

When she headed toward the stairs, a bright spot on the hardwood floor drew her attention. In fact, the foyer's floor was splattered with whatever it was. She bent to touch one, and her fingertip came away sticky. And white.

She hurried to the wall, and when she flipped the light switch the odor hit her. She'd been smelling it since she left her quarters, but hadn't paid attention because she'd been so focused on finding the cat. The smell was unmistakably that of paint. She lifted her finger and sniffed. Yes, definitely paint. And unless she was very much mistaken, not white paint. Beige.

Fear struck her like an open hand. The paint had been stacked in Sew Welcome, the cans still sealed. Her fingers tightened around the flashlight. Then how did paint get splattered out here?

Holding Frank close, she followed the trail of paint drops into the rotunda. The smell was stronger there. The splotches led to the left and ended at the entrance of Sew Welcome.

Swallowing hard, Liz tiptoed in that direction. The shop's door was closed. She did not touch it, in case the police needed to dust for fingerprints. Instead, she pressed her forehead against the glass and strained to see inside the dark interior.

What she saw sent her racing for the telephone.

12

"Makes no sense."

Stan Houghton stood in the center of Sew Welcome shaking his head while he surveyed the damage. The paint cans, which had previously rested on the floor, had been moved to the craft table, their lids pried off, and the contents dumped. Paint had spread across the table and had run over the sides in rivers to create giant puddles on the floor. A pair of scissors—presumably the tool used to open the cans—lay covered in the viscous stuff. Four bolts of fabric, which had been selected for the Christmas quilt, were ruined.

Liz had phoned Stan first, and then placed a call to Mary Ann. The co-owner of Sew Welcome arrived within minutes looking as fresh and put-together as if she'd dressed for an evening on the town.

Stan fixed a stare on Mary Ann after she'd looked around. "Are you sure nothing's missing?"

Mary Ann shook her head. "I haven't taken an inventory, but I don't see anything obvious missing. The petty cash is still in the lock box."

"Nothing gone from the house?" Stan inquired of Liz.

"Not that I've seen." After the phone calls, Liz had deposited Frank in the library, shut the door, and then done a quick walk-through of the inn's main floor. "I haven't inspected the guest rooms, of course, but I don't see so much as coffee pod missing from the downstairs rooms I've checked."

Stan's thumbs flew across the screen of his phone as he tapped notes. "Have you checked all the windows and doors for signs of forced entry?"

At the idea of someone breaking into the inn, a sick flutter erupted in Liz's stomach. "Only the front door, when I let you two in."

Without a word Stan strode away. Liz and Mary Ann exchanged a glance and then hurried after him. After pulling on a pair of rubber gloves, he tested the locks on every window and every door. The three-person parade filed through each room of the first floor, ending back at the entrance to Sew Welcome. Stan knelt before the door, pulled a small penlight from his pocket, and shone the beam on the lock.

"Hard to say for sure, but I think this one has been picked."

Liz and Mary Ann peered over his shoulders.

"How do you know?" Liz asked.

"Fresh scratches on the metal there and there. See 'em?"

Now that he pointed them out, Liz did see several markings on the handle.

"That means this was a professional job?" Mary Ann asked.

He snapped a few pictures with his phone. "Not necessarily. Anybody in the world can learn how to pick a lock in a matter of minutes. There are dozens of videos online." He sounded disgusted. Standing, he gave Liz a direct look. "Since there's no sign of forced entry from outside the inn, you realize what this means?"

Feeling slightly nauseous, she nodded. "It had to be one of my guests. And I think we all know who."

Mary Ann said what they were all thinking. "Gavin Younger."

"Remember how startled he was yesterday when he saw those paint cans in there?" Liz asked Mary Ann, who nodded. Liz looked at Stan. "If he had stolen the paint, I could understand. He told us he bought it to do some painting in his aunt's house for her. But why would he vandalize Sew Welcome?"

The police chief shrugged. "Regardless, I think it's time we asked him." He gestured toward the staircase. "Lead on."

"You two go ahead." Mary Ann pulled a cell phone from her pocket. "I need to call Sadie and give her the bad news."

After a sidetrack to get the master key from her quarters, Liz climbed the stairs with legs that felt weighed down with lead. Gavin had been out with Kiera last night. What had happened during their casual date to upset him enough to come back and do this kind of damage?

Rounding the second-floor landing, she thrust the thought away. It was too early to call Kiera now, but at eight o'clock on the dot she would get the girl on the phone and ask what had happened last night. She'd also give her a heads-up that Stan would probably want to talk to her.

They reached the third floor and, moving quietly so as not to disturb Caleb, Liz approached the Sunrise Room. She rapped quietly with a knuckle.

"Gavin?"

No answer. She knocked again with the same result. With a glance at Stan, who nodded, she unlocked the door and backed up. The police chief turned the knob and pushed the door open. He started to enter, but then stopped.

"He's not here." His head swiveled as he inspected the room. "No sign of him."

Liz followed him inside. Gavin's duffel bag lay on the upholstered chair near the window, unzipped and the rumpled contents spilling out. Wrinkles in the bedspread indicated that someone had sat on the foot of the bed, but the pillows had not been disturbed. No one had slept here.

Stan snapped a picture of the duffel bag and the bedspread. "Did you hear him come in last night?"

She thought back. She'd heard several sets of footsteps on the staircase while reading her novel in bed, but whose? "I don't know."

"He went out with Kiera Williams last night, didn't he?"

Her stomach gave a queasy flip-flop as she nodded.

"He must have come back sometime and left on foot. I saw his car when I got here." He stopped. "I'm gonna need to talk to Miss Williams. You got her number?"

"Yes, it's—" She was in the act of pulling out her cell phone when her gaze stumbled over the door of the shared bathroom between the Sunrise and Sunset Rooms, which was shut. "Maybe we should check in there."

Stan crossed the hallway. Liz followed on tiptoe, mindful of her sleeping guests on the floor below and Caleb next door. Stan tapped quietly on the wood with a gloved finger, and when he received no answer, twisted the knob and pushed the door open. Breath caught in her chest, Liz was almost afraid to look.

"Nothing in here," Stan said.

The breath left her lungs in a whoosh.

"Who's in that room?" He pointed toward the door to the Sunset Room.

"Caleb Porter, a young man whose parents are in the room directly below."

"I'm going to need to talk to him too. Chances are he heard something, since his door's open."

"What?" Liz pushed past. Sure enough, the door to the Sunset Room stood ajar as well. "That door should be shut and locked. I've spoken to him about that."

"In that case, I *definitely* need to talk to him."

Stan pushed the door open and stuck his head in. Liz gnawed at a fingernail, a dark sense of unease ballooning. What would the Porters think of the police waking their son at three thirty in the morning to question him about a missing guest?

Stan turned in the doorway, his expression puzzled. "Looks like we have two suspects."

Her jaw slack, Liz sidestepped him to enter the room. Like Gavin's, Caleb's bed was empty and undisturbed.

"I—I don't understand." A sense of numbness crept over her. "They don't even know each other. What's going on, Stan?"

"I don't know, but we're going to find out." Looking grim, Stan held up his phone and began snapping pictures.

Liz scanned the room. Unlike Gavin's, the room held no personal effects. Of course, Eunice had unpacked Caleb's suitcase and put his clothing in the dresser. She circled the foot of the bed and extended a hand to open a drawer.

"Wait!" Stan hurried to her side and held up his gloved hand. "Just to be on the safe side." He slid the drawer open and Liz peered inside.

Nothing. The drawer was empty, as were the others.

"I don't understand. I saw his mother put his clothes in here." She turned in a full circle, looking for a suitcase that was not there.

Then she saw something. Or rather, nothing.

"It's gone." She barely managed a whisper.

Stan watched her closely. "What's gone?"

"The lamp I bought from Louise Younger's estate. It's been stolen."

Otis opened the door to the Rose of Sharon Room and glared into the hallway at Liz. "This is an outrage. Do you know what time it is?" He made a show of examining his wrist, and then appeared to realize he wore no watch. "What time *is* it, anyway?"

"It's about quarter to four." Liz poured apology into her voice. "I'm terribly sorry, but I have some very bad news that can't wait."

From behind him, Eunice sat up in the bed, her hair pointing all directions of the compass. "Bad news? Is it a fire?"

Liz glanced over her shoulder. Stan dipped a nod for her to continue.

"The inn has been vandalized." She bit her lip and tried to prepare herself. "And Caleb isn't in his room."

"What?" The woman's screech pierced the air. She launched herself out of bed, ran across the room, and jerked her husband out of the doorway. "My son is missing?"

"Yes, ma'am, we—"

Liz was shoved back as Eunice raced past her and mounted the stairs two at a time, shouting at the top of her lungs. "Caleb? Caleb, where are you?"

Though the rest of the guests would need to be awakened soon, Liz preferred that they not be alarmed by the woman's panicked screeching. She hurried after the frantic mother, who burst through the doorway and then stopped dead in the center of the area rug. Her mouth dangled open as she surveyed the spotless bedroom.

Stan entered at a more sedate pace. "Don't touch anything, please."

"What?" She whirled. "Who are you?"

Liz performed a quick introduction. "This is Stan Houghton, Pleasant Creek's chief of police. I called him when I discovered that the inn had been vandalized."

Otis spoke from the hallway. "You don't suspect Caleb, do you?"

"Of course they don't," his wife snapped. "Our boy wouldn't do anything like that."

When Stan remained silent, Liz rushed to answer. "Of course not. We came upstairs to question Mr. Younger and discovered them both missing."

Eunice whirled on her. "This is *your* fault! If you had given us the room we reserved months ago, none of this would be happening."

Guilt pricked Liz's conscience. The accusation was valid. Not that she regretted giving the unhappy young man a bit of privacy, but why had she put Gavin up here with him? She'd felt sorry for him, yes. And she'd more or less been forced into renting Gavin the room by Betty. But in her heart she knew her reasons went beyond that. If Gavin had any information about his aunt's death, she'd hoped to pry it out of him. Her sleuthing tendencies had overcome good sense.

She was saved from apologizing when Stan's low, rational voice took command. "If there's any evidence to be found in here, we need to leave before we destroy it. Let's go downstairs." He glanced at Liz. "May we use your living room?"

What could she say? She gulped and nodded.

Before Stan commandeered her living room, Liz took the opportunity to throw on a pair of jeans and a sweater, and then dragged Beans from beneath the coffee table. "Remember what I said," she told the shivering animal. "You're a *dog*. Act like one."

The dog slunk away, and Liz regretted her hard tone. At the moment she felt like creeping after him and joining him in a corner.

She found Mary Ann in the kitchen making coffee.

"Put an extra scoop in the filter," Liz told her. "I think we all need to be super alert this morning."

Mary Ann complied. "Sadie will be here shortly."

"What did she say when you told her about the paint?"

Her features scrunched. "I can't repeat talk like that."

Despite herself, Liz chuckled. It took no imagination at all to guess the outspoken Sadie's reaction. "Stan said we can't start cleaning until the evidence team finishes in there."

The water began to drip, and the head-clearing aroma of coffee filled the kitchen. Eyes closed, Liz took a deep breath and formed a silent prayer for Caleb's safety. If anything happened to that young man—

Another worry rose to the forefront of her mind. Kiera. She glanced at the clock. Not quite five. No doubt Stan would finish questioning the guests here before heading to Kiera's mother's house, but Liz's tense stomach muscles couldn't wait that long. She slid her cell phone out of her pocket.

Mary Ann gave her a knowing look as she scrolled through her contacts list. "Kiera?"

Nodding, Liz pressed the call button. *Rrring. Rrring. Rrring.* The knots in her gut tightened. *Please answer. Please.*

"'Lo?" At the sound of Kiera's sleepy voice, Liz wilted against the counter.

"Thank goodness you're okay."

A low-pitched grumble answered. "You called me in the middle of the night to tell me you're glad I'm okay?"

"Gavin didn't come home last night, so I was worried about you."

"That jerk." Now irritation saturated the girl's voice. "We were halfway through our burgers when he got a phone call and went outside to take it. Never came back. He stuck me with the bill." Her voice sounded a bit more alert. "You were so right about him, Liz."

"I'm sorry. I hoped I was wrong. At least his car is here, so he didn't have an accident."

"Oh. I didn't think of that." A moment of subdued silence followed.

"Stan Houghton's here now. He's going to want to talk to you when he finishes questioning everyone here."

"What?" Now the girl sounded fully awake. "What's wrong?"

"The inn was vandalized last night. We discovered Gavin and one other guest missing when we went upstairs to question him about it."

"I'm so sorry! Do you need me to come over?"

A tender smile curved Liz's lips. "Thanks, but Mary Ann is here, and Sadie's on her way. We'll be fine."

"Okay, but tell Chief Houghton I'm heading back to school around lunchtime. And if you change your mind, give me a call."

"I will. Drive safely, Kiera."

Liz disconnected the call and stared at the phone a long moment. Thankfully Kiera was safe. But what of Caleb? Had he gotten mixed up with Gavin and left with him? But that didn't explain why Caleb's clothes were missing while Gavin's were still in the Sunrise Room.

At least they hadn't driven anywhere, so they were on foot. Unless Gavin had reconnected with some of the unsavory friends from his high school days and introduced Caleb to them.

Why, oh why, had she rented Gavin a room?

13

Maddox accepted a cup of coffee from Mary Ann. "I don't know about anyone else, but I didn't hear a thing. Slept like a rock all night."

He stood at the kitchen counter stirring sugar into his mug while the other members of the Three Eagles nodded their agreement. The trio had responded to the early morning wake-up call much more pleasantly than the Porters. But then again everyone in their party was present and accounted for. Donnie yawned repeatedly and Phil slumped in a kitchen chair, his hands cupping a steaming mug and his eyes half shut.

Stan maintained a pleasant expression. "If it's all right with you, I'd still like to speak with each of you privately."

Was it Liz's imagination or did Phil's grip on the mug tighten? Without a doubt, she intercepted a look that passed between Maddox and Donnie, though it was too quick to interpret.

"Of course." Maddox set down the spoon and picked up his coffee. "I won't be much help, but I'm happy to answer your questions."

The other two voiced their agreement as well.

"Thank you. I won't take much of your time." Stan addressed Maddox. "I'll start with you, if that's okay. Please follow me."

The two disappeared into Liz's quarters, and the door closed behind them. Liz hesitated, torn between a desire to support Mary Ann when Sadie arrived at Sew Welcome and saw the mess, and her duty as an innkeeper. Duty won out, and she slid into a chair at the kitchen table.

"I'm so sorry for this disruption to your weekend of rest."

Phil dismissed the apology with a flip of his hand. "We're good. The ones I feel sorry for are Eunice and Otis. To have your kid turn up missing . . ." He shook his head.

Liz could not banish the image of Eunice's blotchy red face, tears streaming, as the police officer Stan had summoned helped her into the cruiser for the short drive down to headquarters. Thankfully, Indiana had no waiting period before filing a missing person's report.

"I hope they find him and Gavin before . . ." A lump rose in her throat, which she attempted to wash down with a sip of lukewarm coffee.

"Yeah." Phil grimaced to indicate she didn't have to finish the sentence. "Me too."

She switched her gaze to Donnie, who was beginning to look more alert. "You didn't hear anything all night?"

He jerked upright in the chair, eyes darting around the room and looking like a schoolboy caught peeking at his neighbor's test paper. "Me? Why would I hear anything?"

Interesting reaction. Liz schooled her expression. "Since the Somewhere in Time Room is located directly above Sew Welcome, I thought you might have heard a commotion downstairs."

"Oh." The guilt evaporated. "I sleep with earplugs. I'm a super-light sleeper, and Maddox snores like a freight train. That's why I insisted on getting the room by myself."

"It's more like a jackhammer." Phil smiled ruefully. "Just my luck to get stuck rooming with him."

Yet another reason Liz's decision to rent a room to Gavin had been a mistake. If only she'd kept to her original plan, the Three Eagles would each have had a room to themselves, and Caleb would not be missing.

Speaking of freight trains, a human imitation charged into the kitchen at that moment. Had steam puffed from Sadie's nostrils, Liz would not have been surprised.

"Where is that delinquent?" she snarled, her hands clenched into fists. "I'm going to pound him!"

"If you mean Gavin, he isn't here. Apparently he left in the middle of the night." Liz rose to retrieve a coffee cup and Sadie's favorite peppermint mocha creamer from the fridge.

"Probably afraid to be here when we found his handiwork, and rightly so." She accepted the cup, filled it halfway with coffee and topped it off with creamer all the way to the rim. "Have you seen that mess? Six bolts of fabric, ruined! Not to mention the cost of cleaning up the place. The area rug will have to be replaced and the hardwoods might have to be refinished if they can't be cleaned. And think of the time we'll lose." She stirred with such vigor that coffee sloshed over the rim.

"It might not have been Gavin." Liz spoke in a rational tone to counteract Sadie's fury. "Did Mary Ann tell you that Caleb is missing too?"

"It was Gavin all right, and there's no telling what he's done to that poor boy. Thank the good Lord our Kiera had sense enough to dump him before something terrible happened to her too."

Liz would have corrected her, but the door to her quarters opened. Maddox emerged, followed by Stan.

"Thank you, Mr. Pulliam. Is it okay to call you if I think of further questions?"

Maddox shrugged. "Of course. Anything to help."

Stan's gaze rested on Phil. "If you're ready, Mr. . . ."

Phil gulped as he stood. "Chesser."

"Right this way, sir." Stan ushered him from the room.

When the door closed, Liz refilled Maddox's cup from the carafe.

"What did you tell him?" Donnie asked.

The bigger man shrugged. "The truth. We stopped for a burger after fishing all day, then came back here. Didn't see anyone, so we took showers and went to bed."

Was it Liz's imagination, or did Donnie wear the expression of someone trying to commit a story to memory?

Ridiculous. I'm just jumpy, and no wonder.

"What'd you do with the fish?" Sadie asked.

The two turned startled looks on her.

Donnie answered. "Uh, we didn't have any."

Apparently Liz wasn't the only one who thought the answer was, well, *fishy*. Sadie cocked her head sideways and stared at the big man with narrowed eyes, the perfect imitation of a human lie detector.

"I never heard of anybody fishing for two solid days on any of the lakes in this area without hooking a single fish," Sadie said. "Why, I catch a mess of panfish every time I toss a worm in."

Maddox's smile broadened.

"Of course we caught fish. Panfish for sure, but also bass, so many I couldn't begin to count 'em." He turned to Donnie. "Did you keep count?"

Though he wore a deer-in-the-headlights stare, Donnie shook his head. "Didn't even try."

"We're catch-and-release fishermen," Maddox explained, his smile not dimming a fraction. "You should have seen the one Donnie got. Biggest bass I ever saw."

Donnie's chest swelled, as would any fisherman having landed a beauty of a bass, but Sadie continued to look skeptical.

"Sounds like a fishy story to me." But she chuckled to take the sting out of the accusation and then turned to Liz. "The police lab folks just left. They got all the pictures they want, so Mary Ann and I are going home to put on some old duds and start cleaning up. I'll bring something to see if we can get those paint spots off your floor."

"Thanks, Sadie."

Liz watched her go. Given the choice, she'd much rather join in the cleanup effort than tackle the next thing on her to-do list—wake Betty Lewis and inform her the chief of police wanted to question her. But there was no way around the unpleasant task.

She emptied the remains of her coffee into the sink and turned to head for the stairs—and nearly fell over Beans. He stood at her feet, staring up at her with a mournful expression.

"What's wrong, boy?"

In answer, he turned his head and cast a doleful look toward the shiny food dish shelf. A wave of compassion washed over her. The poor dog had suffered enough in the past few days.

"Oh, all right." She lifted the bowls out of the slots, returned them to their customary positions on the rubber mat, and whisked the offensive shelf out of the way.

Looking somewhat happier—though it was hard to tell with Beans—he gave the water bowl a sniff as though to satisfy himself that it was, in fact, the one of which he approved, and then began to eat his kibble.

"I'll start breakfast in a few minutes," she promised the two guests at her kitchen table.

The grandfather clock in the rotunda reported the time as ten minutes past six. She climbed the stairs, not bothering to walk softly. Maybe her footsteps would do the trick and save her from having to wake the woman.

No such luck. The rumble of a steady snore resounded from behind the door to the Amish Room. Sucking in a breath, Liz rapped on the wood. The snore cut off abruptly, and a muffled voice slurred, "Who's there?"

"Betty, it's Liz." She didn't temper the volume of her voice. Everyone in the house was up already. "I'm sorry to bother you."

"Botherrrrrrr." The response ended with the return of the snore.

Liz knocked again, this time so hard her knuckles stung. "Betty, you need to wake up. Something's happened, and the police want to speak with you."

"Huh? Whazzat?"

"The police," Liz shouted, her lips pressed to the crease between the door and the doorjamb. "They have some questions for you."

The vast squeaking of springs sounded, and a moment later the door swung inward. A blur of black-and-white whizzed past Liz's feet. She barely had time to notice, her attention fixed instead on Betty Lewis's furious face.

"What is the meaning of this?" Outrage boosted the woman's volume, and the question echoed down the stairs. "I *knew* you would be unreasonable when you discovered Frank loose in the house, but I never *dreamed* you'd lock him up and contact the authorities."

Laughter threatened, both at the ludicrous idea of calling the police on a cat and at the voluminous nightshirt emblazoned with a cartoon bird that Liz would never have pictured the haughty woman wearing. She managed to control her mirth and offer an explanation.

"I'm afraid the situation is far more serious than that. The inn has been vandalized, and two guests are missing."

Betty's nostrils flared several times as she digested the news. "I don't see what that has to do with me. Surely the police's questions can wait until a decent hour."

"I'm truly sorry." Liz pasted on a mollifying smile. "But the situation is urgent. One of those missing is Caleb Porter."

Her eyes widened. "Eunice's boy? Why, the poor woman must be beside herself." She glanced around the hallway and went on in a whisper. "Are they dragging the lake?"

Though Liz had considered the possibility that Caleb was dead, the idea of his body surfacing from the depths of beautiful Jaynes Lake sent a shiver through her frame.

"I hope that won't be necessary. His clothes and suitcase are gone too."

"Ah." She gave a knowing nod. "Ran away, then. When I first met him I thought he had the look of a young man who was being strangled by his mother's apron strings."

Liz blinked. Why in the world hadn't she thought of that? Caleb had run away. That made far more sense than him getting sucked into Gavin's web.

As for Gavin, he had probably come back to the inn late, spied the paint cans through the windows of Sew Welcome, and been overcome by thoughts of his aunt's demise. Not knowing how to handle his grief or anger, he'd engaged in a paint-dumping session, then bolted without his things rather than risk being caught sneaking up to the third floor. And he wouldn't have taken his car for fear that the sound would wake the others. *Obviously.*

She rubbed at her eyes. Obviously she'd been too sleep deprived to have seen the obvious. The disappearances of two of her guests could be totally unrelated.

"Be sure to mention that to Stan Houghton when you talk to him." She eyed Betty's nightshirt. "Um, I'm sure you have time to get dressed first."

Liz descended the stairs in a much lighter mood. The explanation made perfect sense. Gavin would turn up soon—to retrieve his car, if nothing else—and if Stan sent some of his officers to question the residents of Pleasant Creek, no doubt someone would report seeing Caleb carrying his suitcase down the road late last night, probably heading for the interstate to hitch a ride to Fort Wayne and the nearest train or bus station. Nobody was dead.

Her foot stumbled on the last step.

Nobody except Louise Younger.

Gavin couldn't have killed her. But then who did?

Well, that was a matter for the Fort Wayne police, not her.

In the kitchen she discovered that Stan had finished talking with Phil and was now closeted with Donnie. She refreshed Maddox's and Phil's coffee and, when she turned, her eyes snagged on a black-and-white figure stretched out in front of Beans's nearly-full food bowl. Frank blinked up at her.

"You are a naughty kitty." She scooped up the cat. "But I know how to keep you occupied, at least long enough for Beans to eat."

With the cat draped across one arm, she retrieved a container of cream from the fridge and poured some into a small bowl. With a grin at Maddox and Phil, she carried both cat and cream to the utility room and deposited them on the floor.

"There. Enjoy the treat. I'll let you out when Beans has finished his breakfast."

She closed the door on a delighted Frank, who purred as he lapped at the cream, and returned to the kitchen. Beans had emerged from wherever he'd been sulking, and she stooped to give his ear a good rub, then turned to eye the fridge. The morning's chaos had left her itching to cook something special and complicated—a sure-fire stress reliever, as she would be too focused on creating a culinary masterpiece to think about anything else.

"Do you like smoked salmon?" she asked as she passed through the kitchen on her way to the four-season room.

Her guests' faces brightened, and they nodded with enthusiasm.

"Good. Eggs Benedict with salmon coming right up."

The chive plant on the windowsill of the four-season room had flourished since being transplanted from the herb garden outside. Liz pinched off several stalks and paused to inhale the fresh scent. Her gaze strayed beyond the window, to the inky surface of Jaynes Lake. Though the sun wouldn't rise for another hour or so, already the eastern horizon betrayed signs of its approach. The nearly full moon hung low over the lake and painted the back lawn in a calming white light. Unable to resist a moment's escape, she unlocked the door and slipped outside. Goose bumps rose on her arms, but she drew in a deep, chilly breath, willing the cold to clear her head. A slight breeze blew across the lake and delivered the comforting scent of water. Her gaze strayed that way.

She did a double-take. Was that an animal perched on one arm of the bench? Narrowing her eyes, she squinted in the dim light. A raccoon, maybe? She took a couple of steps in that direction. Whatever it was, it didn't move.

As she neared, more of the form came into focus. Something—correction, some*one* lay on the bench, his or her head propped on the metal arm. Was it Gavin?

She moved faster, fury building with every step. "Gavin, is that you?"

She rounded the edge of the gazebo and stood over him. Her body cast a deep shadow over his, but the moonlight shone on his face. It was Gavin, all right. One arm dangled off the bench, the sleeve of his jacket and his hand covered in beige paint. So this is where he'd decided to sleep after wrecking Sew Welcome.

Planting her hands on her hips, she shouted, "Gavin, wake up!"

He didn't move. She bent over to shove him. "I said wake—"

Her hand touched something wet, and cold, and sticky. Paint, no doubt. Drawing back, she extended her arm so the moonlight shone on the thick liquid covering her palm. Black? Correction. Not black. Red.

Blood red.

Her shriek shattered the stillness of the early morning.

14

"I don't believe it, not for a minute." Mary Ann, wearing rubber gloves and a paint-splattered shirt, held open a garbage bag for Liz to deposit a bolt of spoiled fabric. "That young man didn't have a violent bone in his body."

Sadie, on her hands and knees in the shop's entryway scrubbing at the paint trail, looked up. "She has a point. From what you say, if Caleb had a tendency toward violence he would have strangled his mother by now."

"I agree." When Mary Ann gave Liz a startled look, she amended her comment. "About Caleb not being violent, not about strangling his mother. I'm just saying that's the conclusion Stan is bound to come to. Caleb packed his bags and disappeared the same night Gavin was murdered. That's too suspicious to be a coincidence."

"Do *you* think he did it?" Sadie asked.

"No." Thoughts whirled in Liz's brain. Of course Caleb hadn't killed Gavin. But Gavin was dead, and Caleb was missing. With his luggage.

Naomi, who had been summoned for an emergency supply of sweet rolls to serve the inn's guests, wore more worry lines on her normally smooth brow than Beans did. "Personally, I'm worried about Caleb. He came by Sweet Everything yesterday afternoon and bought a dozen napoleons. I chatted with him for a few minutes. He seemed like a nice, level-headed young man."

A dozen napoleons? That solved the mystery of why he'd been late for coffee hour. He'd been walking around the lake stuffing himself on sweets that his mother would no doubt disapprove of.

A powerful ache pounded inside Liz's skull. It had begun with the discovery of Gavin's body and continued to intensify in the ensuing two hours. It seemed as if Stan had summoned the entire Pleasant Creek police force. A dozen officers, both in uniform and in plain clothes, filled the inn and the back lawn. Cameras flashed, paint drops were measured, black fingerprint dust covered every door and window. The guests had been rushed through breakfast and then asked politely to stay out of the way. They'd all returned to their rooms, Betty clutching Frank as though she feared he'd become the next victim.

The lemon scent of the cleaner Sadie was applying to the hardwood floor blended with that of paint. The overpowering combination was probably making Liz's headache worse. She took the sealed garbage bag from Mary Ann and piled it beside the others, then began opening the windows along the front wall.

Mary Ann followed suit. "Good idea. It wouldn't do to asphyxiate ourselves on top of everything else."

The window open, Liz lingered to stare outside. The sight of yellow police tape strung across the inn's front porch sent a sick feeling to the pit of her stomach. Across the street, a small group of gawkers had gathered. Among them she spied the red head of Rob Carver, a reporter for the *Pleasant Creek News & Views*. As if that wasn't bad enough, a white van pulled up to the front curb with an immediately recognizable logo on the side.

"Oh my." From her position at the center window, Mary Ann turned a sympathetic look her way. "It's Channel 12."

Liz groaned. One of the television stations from Fort Wayne. They'd certainly wasted no time in appearing.

"We're going to be on TV?" Sadie jumped up and ran to the third window, peeling off her gloves and smoothing her hair.

Mary Ann gave her a disapproving frown.

"What?" Sadie splayed her hands. "This could be a big boost for business. You know what they say. Any publicity is good publicity."

Naomi came to stand beside Liz. "I think having a guest murdered on your property is an exception to the rule."

"Nonsense. It's not like *we* killed him."

The four of them watched as the van door slid open and a recognizable blonde woman emerged.

"It's Kelly Chapman." Sadie practically danced in place. "I watch her every night."

Another figure exited the van, a young man with long hair and a giant camera perched on his shoulder. Kelly Chapman glanced up and down the street and, clutching a microphone in her hand, strode across with a confident step. Rob Carver separated himself from the watchers and hurried after her.

"How in the world does Kelly walk in those things?" Mary Ann wondered aloud.

Liz spared a glance at the reporter's heels, which must have been at least four inches high, then focused on Officer George Hughes standing guard on the sidewalk in front of the inn. At Ms. Chapman's approach, he spread his feet shoulder width apart and clasped his hands behind his back. He might have presented an official, military-like appearance if not for the huge bulge of his stomach overhanging his belt. Their voices drifted through the open windows, but Liz couldn't make out the words.

"He won't let her in." A note of approval sounded in Mary Ann's voice.

"Ha!" Sadie said.

George shook his head, and Ms. Chapman folded her arms, still clutching the microphone. Her head lifted as she inspected the exterior of the inn, and then she gestured for the camera operator to follow.

She walked a few yards away from George and came to a stop on the sidewalk just outside the sitting room. The young man stepped out into the street and pointed the camera at her. Rob hovered behind him, his pen flying across the pages of a notebook.

"She's broadcasting." Sadie turned a delighted grin on Liz. "Aren't you glad you had the inn's sign repainted this summer?"

Liz didn't answer, but strained to hear the reporter. Since the woman faced the opposite direction, she caught only a few words, but they were enough. "Pleasant Creek . . . local establishment . . . murder." Liz cringed, and Naomi winced in sympathy.

Rob caught sight of them. His gaze locked onto Liz, and she sucked in a breath as she stepped back. Too late.

"Ms. Eckardt!" the red-headed reporter shouted. Clutching his notebook, he approached the window at something just short of a run. "Would you care to make a statement?"

Kelly Chapman stopped speaking mid-sentence to turn toward the window.

Rob, who had left the sidewalk and hopped over an azalea, tossed a comment over his shoulder. "Liz Eckardt owns the Olde Mansion Inn."

Ms. Chapman told the camera operator, "Keep it rolling." Displaying an agility Liz wouldn't have thought possible in four-inch heels and a straight skirt, she followed Rob over the ornamental shrubs lining the sidewalk.

From his position on the porch, the officer realized what was going on and raced down the walkway, shouting, "Hey! You can't go there."

The reporters ignored him. Rob came right up to the center window and stuck his head near to the screen to shout inside. "Ms. Eckardt, is it true you found a body on your property?"

"Don't say a word!" Officer Hughes yelled, moving toward them as quickly as his girth permitted.

Liz didn't answer, and Rob turned his head slightly so his voice was clearly overheard by the television reporter and her cameraman. "This isn't the first time the Olde Mansion Inn has been implicated in a murder investigation. Care to make a statement about that, Ms. Eckardt?"

Implicated? He made it sound as if guests were strangled in their beds at the inn on a regular basis. That came close to a libelous accusation. Liz clenched her jaw to keep from responding.

Ms. Chapman pushed her face close to the screen beside Rob's. "Can you verify that a murder has occurred on this property?"

George Hughes arrived, his face red and his breath heaving. "This is an open investigation. Chief Houghton will make an official statement when he's ready."

Liz grasped the top of the window and slammed it down. Mary Ann did the same and then hurried over to shut the one in front of Sadie. Outside, the officer ushered the two reporters and the cameraman back to the sidewalk. Just before she pulled down the shade, Liz saw Kelly Chapman speak into her microphone and then extend the instrument toward Rob while the camera focused on the two of them. *Terrific.* Rob would leap at the chance to be interviewed on television.

Sadie stood with her face plastered to the glass. "That glory hog is going to be on Channel 12." Disappointment colored her tone.

Placing a hand on her shoulder, Mary Ann pulled her back and closed the shade. "I think we all need a break. If the police are through in the sitting room, let's go in there and have a cup of coffee."

"Good idea." Naomi put a comforting arm around Liz. "You need to eat something."

Maybe some food in her stomach would help her headache. Liz shut her eyes, but the image of Gavin's body haunted her. She shook her head. "I don't think I can eat, but coffee sounds good."

The four left the shop. The clearer air in the rotunda had an immediate effect on the pounding in Liz's head, and she inhaled a deep breath.

Footsteps on the stairs alerted them to the approach of the Three Eagles, who descended carrying their suitcases.

Maddox caught sight of them. "Glad you're here, Ms. Eckardt. We're taking off." He extended a hand holding their room keys.

The Material Girls disappeared into the sitting room as Liz accepted the keys. "I'm so sorry your relaxing weekend ended this way."

"That's not your fault. This is a great place."

Stan entered from the kitchen. He took in the scene, his gaze pausing when it lit on the duffel bag dangling from Maddox's hand. "I'm sorry, gentlemen, but you can't leave."

The three exchanged startled glances.

"What do you mean?" Phil's clutch on the handle of his rolling suitcase tightened.

"A man has been murdered." Stan gave them a tight-lipped smile. "Until everyone has been cleared, nobody leaves town."

Thoughts ricocheted madly in Liz's mind. Did Stan suspect these three were somehow involved in Gavin's murder? She had guests checking in this afternoon. If the Three Eagles couldn't leave, there would be no room for the newcomers. Well, except for the two vacancies on the third floor, but those were singles and wouldn't accommodate her new guests. And if these three couldn't leave, did that mean Betty couldn't check out either?

But she knew how the legal process worked, and she'd known Stan long enough to trust him, so she held her tongue. Though it would mean a loss of income, she'd call the nearby Crystal Lake Inn or a local motel and see if they could accommodate her guests.

Maddox's chest inflated, his expression belligerent. "We've already told you everything we know."

"About the vandalism. Not about the murder."

Phil's face flushed an angry red. "We don't know anything about that."

Donnie nodded. "And we have to go back to work tomorrow."

Stan's smile took on a chill. "We'll do the best we can to rush the process, but background checks and so on take time. I expect you'll be able to leave by tomorrow."

"Background checks?" Phil's voice echoed up to the rotunda's domed ceiling. "Are we suspects?"

"At this point, everyone is. Standard procedure."

Phil bristled. "I can't stay until tomorrow. I don't have any more vacation time."

The police chief's expression became stony. "I can make a call to your supervisor if that will help."

Phil's eyes narrowed, and Stan continued to hold his gaze in what threatened to become an uncomfortable staring contest.

Maddox stepped between the two men. "Are we confined to this inn?"

"You're not under house arrest. I'll need you to go down to headquarters and file official statements about any connection you may have with the victim."

"We don't have any connections with him," Donnie said.

"This is ridiculous," Phil snapped. "You can't keep us here against our will."

A hint of steel appeared in Stan's features. "If necessary, I can arrange accommodations in the county jail. Legally I can hold you for obstruction of justice." His voice left no doubt that he would follow through on the threat.

Donnie broke the tension. "Hey, we'll do whatever we can to help." He glanced at Phil. "Of course we will."

Maddox nodded, then turned to Liz. "Guess we'll need those keys back."

She handed them over and stepped to Stan's side to watch the three carry their luggage back upstairs. When the sound of a closing door echoed down, she faced him.

"Do you know something about them?"

He continued to stare after the trio. "They're involved. I'm sure of it. I just don't know how yet."

"What makes you think so?"

His gaze flickered toward her. "I can't say."

Lawyer Liz understood the need for law enforcement to keep mum with information in an investigation. Though she had a hard time believing the likable Maddox would be involved in any way with an unsavory person like Gavin, she herself had entertained questions about the singing group.

"What about Betty Lewis? Are you going to let her leave?" She didn't bother asking about the Porters. With their son missing, dynamite wouldn't get them to budge from Pleasant Creek, and she didn't blame them.

He scratched the back of his neck, apparently considering the question. "She could probably leave, but I'd have to come up with a plausible explanation as to why she could leave and the others can't. I'd rather she stay until tomorrow."

Great. That would go over with the prickly woman like a floating brick. An ugly idea crept into Liz's mind. She lowered her voice. "Are the rest of us in danger?"

He pursed his lips. "I don't think so," he said finally. "But I'm going to leave a few uniforms here just in case."

Police inside the inn, reporters outside, and a body in the gazebo. The pain in her head pounded with renewed energy. She rubbed her temples and managed a weak, "Thanks."

Stan awarded her a sympathetic grimace. "Don't worry. I'm running a rush check on a couple of things, and if what I suspect is true, those three have some explaining to do. I expect they'll be down at headquarters before night falls."

When Liz entered the sitting room, Naomi pressed a hot coffee mug into her hands. The soothing aroma rose from the contents. With a grateful smile, she sipped, willing the headache to recede.

"Sit down, Liz." Mary Ann patted the couch cushion beside her. "You look pale."

"I can't." Her voice sounded even wearier than she felt. "I've got to find alternate accommodations for the guests who are supposed to check in today, and then call them and let them know."

She explained the latest developments, including Stan's suspicion that the Three Eagles were involved in Gavin's death. Before she finished, Jackson entered the room. He crossed to stand before her, his gaze searching.

"I heard someone was killed." Concern made his voice deeper than normal. "Are you okay?"

Liz gave a weary nod. "How did you find out?"

"I had the TV news on while I was getting ready for church."

"We're on television?" Sadie leaped to her feet. "Already?"

"Liz was, briefly." He grimaced. "And Rob Carver was being interviewed. That's when I left to come over."

"Let's go see."

Sadie charged out of the room, and the others fell in step behind her. Liz started after them, but Jackson stopped her with a hand on her arm.

"Are you sure you're all right?"

"I'm a little shaken, but otherwise fine." She mustered a smile for his benefit. "How bad did it sound on TV?"

"It wasn't good," he admitted. "Rob started reciting a list of previous crimes that have occurred around Pleasant Creek."

"You mean around the inn."

His features scrunched. "Yeah."

With a sigh, Liz headed after the girls. "I'd better watch it. If he's said anything libelous . . ." She left the comment unfinished. Any threat she made would be empty, and they both knew it. Liz was not litigious, even if she *was* a former lawyer. But she needed to see how bad it looked for the Olde Mansion Inn so she could come up with a plan for damage control.

And right now, it certainly didn't look good.

15

Jackson and Stan left the inn together, heading to police headquarters to consult on the official statement to the press. Liz and her friends hovered in the foyer and listened as Stan told those gathered outside that he would hold a news conference at three o'clock on the steps of the courthouse. If he'd hoped his announcement would distract the onlookers from the departure of the coroner's van, he'd miscalculated their attentiveness. The Channel 12 camera operator whirled in time to film the van pulling out of the inn's driveway.

"Have you identified the murder victim?" Ms. Chapman shoved her microphone in Stan's face as he ducked under the yellow police tape.

Liz clearly heard his curt, "No comment."

"Good for him." Sadie's desire to be on television had apparently faded as they'd watched Rob's interview and the Channel 12 anchorwoman's insinuating comments regarding what she called "the latest in a series of criminal activities revolving around Pleasant Creek's Olde Mansion Inn." Sadie folded her arms and glared. "I wouldn't give that woman the time of day if she paid me for it."

The hint of a smile hovered around Mary Ann's lips. "Not even in return for publicity for Sew Welcome?"

Sadie's chin rose. "At the expense of the inn? No ma'am."

Liz felt the weight of Naomi's stare and raised an eyebrow in an unspoken question.

"I think you should lie down and rest for a while. You look like you're about to collapse," Naomi said to Liz.

"She needs to eat something, whether she wants it or not. We all do." Mary Ann looped an arm through hers and guided her to the kitchen.

Liz allowed herself to be deposited into a chair while Naomi rummaged in the fridge. She *did* feel a bit wobbly, no doubt from a combination of shock, worry, and low blood sugar. In fact, if she let her guard down she could probably lay her head on the table and have a good cry. Tears felt dangerously close to the surface.

"I can't help thinking this is my fault." Pain squeezed her throat at the admission.

"That's ridiculous," Sadie said.

"No it's not," Liz insisted. "I should never have let him stay here."

Sadie planted her hands on her hips. "If you're at fault, then so are we. After all, if we'd told you about Leah Schwartz in the first place you would have sent him away."

"She's right." Mary Ann slid into the chair next to Liz. "In fact, if we're throwing blame around, I started the whole thing by suggesting we go to the auction."

Liz covered her hand. "That's just plain silly."

"Exactly." Mary Ann smiled. "So let's have no more talk of that sort. It is what it is."

Naomi emerged from the refrigerator, her hands full of eggs, cheese, and deli ham. "Speaking of the auction, I still think it's odd that the lamp is missing from Caleb's room. Why would he take a lamp?"

"I know what you mean." Liz tapped a finger on the vinyl place mat. "Especially after I caught Gavin getting ready to go into the Sunset Room. I wondered at the time if he was planning to steal the lamp."

"Maybe he did," Sadie said. "Or maybe Caleb stole it for him and then felt so guilty he ran away."

Liz shook her head. The missing lamp was important somehow, but that explanation didn't ring true. Caleb was no more a thief than he was a killer. It just didn't make sense. Nothing did. The lamp. The paint. The—

She stiffened.

Mary Ann eyed her. "What's wrong?"

"Louise's trunk." Liz looked at Sadie. "It was one of the things Gavin wanted so badly. What if he convinced Caleb to give him the lamp, and then in the middle of the night he went looking for the trunk? Since he saw the paint in Sew Welcome, he might have thought he would find the trunk there too."

Sadie looked thoughtful. "Well at least we saved that from him. But if he did steal the lamp, where is it?"

Mary Ann shook her head. "More importantly, why did he want those things so badly? I don't believe for a minute his reason was sentimental."

"Neither do I," Liz said. "What if something was hidden *inside* them?"

Naomi paused in the act of cracking an egg into a bowl. "You mean like money?"

"I don't know. Something valuable enough that after he broke into Sew Welcome and didn't find the trunk, he was so angry he trashed the place with paint out of spite."

"You gals are nuts." Sadie shook her head. "There's nothing in the trunk. We looked."

"What if there's a hidden compartment?" Liz glanced at Mary Ann, who looked thoughtful. "We need to examine that trunk."

When she started to rise, Naomi stopped her with a firm hand on her shoulder. "First, we're all going to eat an omelet. No one has eaten anything, and we need energy to think straight."

Liz saw that it was no use arguing, because they were all nodding. Frustrated, she settled again in her chair.

With her stomach full and her headache thankfully gone, Liz and the others piled into Mary Ann's car for the drive out to Sadie's house. The trunk sat in a corner of the small barn Sadie called her toolshed.

"Should we call Jackson to help?" Liz asked. "He knows about antique furniture and might be able to search it without causing any damage."

"No need." Sadie opened up a tool chest and pulled out a screwdriver. "I checked an online auction site. It's not really an antique, and it isn't worth much." She got down on her knees and went to work on the hinges.

Twenty minutes later the four women stood in a circle, staring down at the tattered remains of Louise Younger's trunk.

"I don't get it." Liz shook her head. "I was sure we'd find something."

With a toe, Mary Ann nudged a strip of yellowed paper that had lined the interior. "Maybe we misjudged Gavin, and he really did just want a memento."

"Nonsense." Sadie bent to gather the hinges they'd removed. "He probably thought it was valuable and he wanted to sell it."

"It's certainly not worth anything now," Naomi said.

Liz winced. "I'm sorry, Sadie."

She dismissed the apology with a wave. "Easy come, easy go."

"Since there's nothing hidden in the trunk, then there probably wasn't anything in the lamp either." Mary Ann tapped a finger on her lips, her stare unfocused. "We're back to square one. But where is the lamp?"

"The bigger question is, where is Caleb?" Naomi's delicious omelet sat uneasily in Liz's stomach. "I have a feeling if we find one we'll find the other."

Liz didn't expect the Porters for coffee hour that afternoon, but they came. Eunice slumped in a chair, her face bearing the ravages of a day full of tears. She clutched a wadded tissue, which she raised often to blot at her eyes. Otis paced the perimeter of the room. Neither touched the plate of cookies, but Eunice did accept a cup of coffee from Liz.

"We've put Caleb's picture in every window in town." Otis plucked at his shirtsleeve as he made a turn by the fireplace. "And that television reporter broadcast the photo and asked anyone with information to call the police."

"She made it sound like Caleb is responsible for that man's death." Eunice's voice broke.

Otis whirled to fix a stern stare on Liz. "If we'd known about all the stuff that's happened around this place we would never have brought our boy here, even for the wedding."

Though her instinct was to bristle, Liz fought to remain calm. The man's son was missing, after all. "I feel terrible about this."

The stare held for a while, and then he scrubbed a hand across his eyes. "I'm sorry. I don't mean to be insulting. I'm just worried."

"Of course you are," Liz said.

Betty entered the sitting room with Frank in her arms. "I've been trying to nap, but my nerves are a fright. And then I nearly had a heart attack when I came out of my room to find the police roaming the halls." She collapsed into the chair opposite Eunice's and began stroking Frank. "It's bad enough being held prisoner here, but must we have guards set on us?"

"They're here for your security," Liz told her.

She jerked upright. "Do we need protection?"

Nothing could induce her to reveal Stan's suspicions regarding the Three Eagles, so she forced a calm smile. "A precaution only."

"Well, this has certainly turned out to be an unpleasant vacation." When she looked at Eunice, pity squeezed her features. "My dear, I'm sure you're beside yourself with worry."

The miserable woman nodded.

An uncomfortable silence threatened, but was broken when Stan stalked into the room. Eunice leaped from her chair and charged toward him, Otis at her side.

"Is there news of Caleb?" Her eyes begged for information.

When he shook his head, Liz had to look away from the anguish in the parents' faces.

"I'm sorry." Stan's tone held so much compassion that tears stung Liz's eyes. "We've questioned nearly everyone in town, but no one has seen him since yesterday afternoon. Don't give up hope, though. Something will turn up."

Eunice buried her face in her husband's shirt, while he patted her back.

Stan caught Liz's eye. "I need to speak with your other guests."

"The Three Eagles?"

He nodded. "They never came to headquarters to file those statements."

"They're upstairs. I think. I haven't seen them since this morning." Liz stood to show him which rooms, but halted when Betty spoke.

"No, they're not. They went out a few hours ago." She stroked Frank. "I haven't heard them return."

"Their car is still in the driveway." A slight tic jerked in Stan's right cheek. "Did they say where they were going?"

"I didn't speak with them," she said. "I saw them through my window. I think they left the house from the back door, because they went behind the garage. I assumed they were taking a stroll along the lake."

Without a word, Stan pivoted on his heel and stalked away. Liz hurried after him. In the rotunda, Officer Hughes sat on a chair, tapping on a cell phone, which he pocketed at his chief's approach.

"Why didn't you follow those three when they left?" Stan snapped.

Hughes looked surprised. "What are you talking about? They haven't gone anywhere. Dixon and I have been here all day."

On the second-floor landing Liz spied the legs of Officer Dixon, who sat in a chair situated to give him a view of every guest's door.

"Dixon," Stan barked up the stairs, and the young man leaped to his feet.

A moment later his face appeared over the railing. "Sir?"

"Those three still in their rooms?"

"Yes, sir. I think they're sleeping. Haven't heard a peep out of them in a few hours."

Tight-lipped, Stan said to Liz, "You want to get your keys?"

She did, and then followed Stan up the stairs, George bringing up the rear. Heading for the Somewhere in Time Room, she told him, "This is Donnie Higgins's room."

But Dixon pointed down the hallway. "They're all three in there."

They trouped to the Heirloom Room and Stan pounded on the door. "This is Chief Stan Houghton. Need to talk to you."

Not a sound came from within.

He tried the knob and then glanced at Liz. "Unlock it."

Both of the other officers unsnapped the straps securing their service revolvers, an act that set Liz's knees trembling. Fingers shaking, she did as requested and then stepped back to allow Stan to swing the door open. Dixon entered first followed by Hughes, both officers' hands resting on their pistol grips.

"They're not here," Hughes said.

Dixon turned to Stan. "Honest, sir, I haven't left my post once."

Liz followed Stan into the room. The Three Eagles' escape route became immediately apparent. A window screen had been removed and lay propped against the back wall. A chilly breeze blew the curtains inward from an open window behind the sofa bed. Stan crossed to peer outside, and Liz knew what he would see—the shingled roof of the patio outside the four-season room below.

Hughes voiced the obvious conclusion. "They must have hopped onto the roof and then dropped to the grass in the backyard."

"They left their stuff." Dixon pointed out two suitcases in the corner.

"Not surprising. If you're on the run you don't weigh yourself down." Stan turned to Liz. "You didn't see or hear anything unusual?"

She shook her head. "We were all out for about an hour not long ago. But otherwise, I've been in Sew Welcome most of the day, helping the girls clean up."

The tic in his cheek twitched. "I need to talk to Ms. Lewis to pinpoint the exact time she saw them. Then I'm going to put out an APB." He glanced at George and Dixon. "You two keep an eye on things here. I'll send someone to relieve you in an hour."

Liz exhaled a pent-up breath. For a moment she'd worried he would remove his officers since the Three Eagles were gone. If they returned for their belongings, she didn't want to face them alone.

"What should I do?" she asked Stan.

"Keep everybody off this floor until the lab techs have had a chance to go over it."

Terrific. Not only were her remaining guests required to stay in Pleasant Creek, now they wouldn't even have access to their rooms for several hours. Betty would pitch a fit.

Night fell with no news of the Three Eagles or Caleb. After an unpleasant two hours of listening to Betty complain and Eunice sniffle, Liz threw her energy into cleaning black fingerprint dust from every surface in the Somewhere in Time and Heirloom Rooms. Then she escaped to her quarters.

When she flipped on the television she was greeted by an unwelcome rerun of Kelly Chapman's morning newscast, followed by a recording of Stan's press conference. The reporters were obviously intrigued to discover that this victim was the nephew of a recent Fort Wayne resident who'd also been stabbed. During the press conference, Jackson stood beside Stan on the courthouse steps, unsmiling and official-looking.

The scene switched back to Kelly in the studio, where she updated the viewing audience on the "gruesome situation unfolding in the seemingly quiet community of Pleasant Creek, with a grisly murder and the disappearance of an eighteen-year-old guest from the Olde Mansion Inn." Teeth grinding, Liz forced herself to watch so she could see if the reporter had gotten wind of the disappearance of three more guests. Thankfully, she had not.

An hour of surfing through mindless television programs revealed nothing worth watching, so Liz gave up and went to bed. Her unfinished novel failed to hold her attention. How could it, when she had a murder mystery unfolding right in her own home? Though the clock read only 8:52, she flipped off the light and arranged herself for sleep.

It did not come.

At eleven o'clock, with the bedsheets hopelessly tangled and her head feeling as if it had been stuffed with cotton, she gave up trying to sleep. Instead, she fired up her laptop. Something had been bothering her, something to do with Gavin. And Leah Schwartz. She couldn't help wondering if Leah would be able to shed light on what was going on here.

And what had happened to her? According to Gavin the couple split up several months ago. Were there hard feelings between them? During the conversation with Mary Ann, Gavin mentioned that Leah was living in "a dump in Indianapolis." Had Gavin contacted her since coming to Indiana for the auction of his aunt's estate?

Half an hour later she'd found Leah Schwartz. No middle name, no phone number, but an address was a good start. The only problem was she'd have to drive to Indianapolis instead of making a phone call. What would Stan say about her leaving town? She tapped a finger on the desk, considering. Her guests had been requested not to leave, but that's because they lived elsewhere and might not return. She'd be gone only a few hours. Sarah wouldn't mind handling the breakfast cleanup, and with Stan's police officers guarding the inn, she didn't have to worry about anything terrible happening in her absence.

The problem justified in her mind, she noted the address on a sticky pad and then clicked over to her email. Maybe she had received something from Steve.

Instead she found a dozen or more new emails, all from former guests. The subject lines almost assaulted her eyes.

Saw the News This Morning.

A Stabbing at the Inn???

Are You Okay?

And one that made her smile: *Kelly Chapman Is a Nitwit.*

Drawing a deep breath for courage, she opened the first and began reading.

Twenty minutes later, she felt much better. Without exception, the emails from the inn's prior guests expressed their support and concern for the situation in which she found herself.

Her cell phone beeped. An incoming text from Steve read, *You awake?*

Grinning, she tapped his number.

"Hey, Mom. I got an email from a buddy in Fort Wayne. What's going on there? Are you okay?"

At the sound of his voice, Liz relaxed against the chair back. A smile she'd been unable to muster all day tickled the corners of her mouth.

"I am now," she said. "It's great to hear your voice."

16

When Liz reached the outskirts of Indianapolis the next morning, she entered the address she'd found on the Internet into her GPS. Lavinia's voice led her through the sprawling suburbs to a narrow street made even more difficult to navigate by a line of cars parked along each curb. Small, single-story houses with almost no yards sat so close together there was barely enough space between them for a person to walk. Grass grew only sparsely in square patches of dirt, and trash littered the sidewalks.

At the end of the street she found the address she sought, a rectangular apartment building made of dingy red brick. The windows had no shutters, and the paint on the front door was hopelessly scarred. Gavin had aptly described this place as a dump. Quite a change from the rolling green hills and fertile fields surrounding the Schwartzes' neat farmhouse back in Pleasant Creek.

Maybe I should have given Leah's address to Stan and let him handle this.

But what would she have said? That she had a feeling Leah might be able to shed some light on Gavin's death? She really had nothing but her gut feeling. If it turned out that Leah did know something, she'd alert Stan the moment she got back home, and she would accept the lecture she would definitely receive in return.

She parked the Acura on the cracked cement of the lot next to the building and then double-checked the locks when she exited. Across the street a woman in a bathrobe stood on her front porch smoking a cigarette. She did not return Liz's friendly wave, but watched her approach the apartment building. The door had a hole where the knob should be, so Liz pushed it open and stepped inside.

The first floor had two apartments on each side of a narrow hallway. A set of rickety-looking stairs led up to a second floor, and Liz spared a grateful thought that she would not need to climb them. Instead, she scanned the numbers on the doors and went to the rear apartment on the right, number 102. Her knock echoed in the empty hallway, and she arranged herself so she could be seen through the peephole.

A female voice came from inside. "Who are you? What do you want?" The familiar Bernese Swiss accent identified the speaker.

Liz pitched her voice to be heard. "My name is Liz Eckardt. I'm looking for Leah Schwartz." She paused and then added, "I'm from Pleasant Creek."

She heard a deadbolt and chain being unlocked, and then the door cracked open. A young woman with a thin face and hollow cheeks came into view. "Did my *Mutter* and *Vater* send you?"

Was that a note of hope in the soft voice?

"No, they didn't. They don't know I'm here."

The girl regarded her with large, solemn eyes. Then, without a word, she swung the door open wide. Liz entered and found herself in a small room with almost no furniture. An efficiency kitchen lay to her right, with a half-sized refrigerator, a two-burner stove, and a sink. The living area contained a couple of mismatched chairs, neither in great condition, and four rusty TV trays. A neat pile of books, including a Bible, rested on the surface of one. A door in the back wall stood open, and through it Liz glimpsed a single bed.

She turned to the girl, noting the dark-blue shirt that seemed to be a uniform. A name tag pinned to her chest bore the logo of a well-known grocery-store chain, and her name. "You're Leah?"

A nod, and the large eyes flickered away from Liz's face. "Will you sit down?"

Liz saw that a book lay open on a tray beside one of the straight-backed chairs, so she settled in the other.

"Would you like a glass of water, or . . ." Leah cast a glance at the refrigerator, "some cheese and crackers?"

Her Amish upbringing showed in the offer. Every visitor to an Amish home, whether expected or not, was treated hospitably, and refreshments were always offered. But this girl didn't look like she had much to spare.

"No, but thank you."

Leah lowered her slender frame onto the other chair and fixed an expectant stare on Liz.

"I'm afraid I have some bad news." Liz spoke softly. "Gavin Younger passed away yesterday."

Leah sucked in a shocked breath. "How? He is—was—young and healthy."

"He was killed. Murdered. Just like his aunt."

"Mrs. Younger?" Tears sprang into the girl's eyes, and she struggled to speak. "But w-why?"

"The police don't know."

"She was a good woman and always kind to me. Even after Gavin and I . . ." She lowered her head and buried her face in her hands, shoulders shuddering with pitiful sobs.

Liz glanced around, and finding no tissue box, went into the bathroom and returned with a roll of toilet paper. She unwound a good portion, handed it to Leah, and then pulled her chair closer so she could place a comforting hand on the young woman's back. "I was hoping you'd be able to tell me something helpful."

Shaking her head, Leah gulped back her tears. "I haven't heard from Gavin in eight months."

"What about before? You . . . stayed with him down in Kentucky, didn't you?"

Her cheeks erupted with fiery spots, but she nodded. "In Radcliff."

"Did he have any enemies?"

"No. Gavin is—" She swallowed. "*Was* friendly to everyone."

"Then what about his friends? Did any of them strike you as odd?" Liz hesitated. "Or dangerous, maybe?"

"I didn't know them." She dabbed at her eyes with the tissue. "He introduced me to a few at first, but I didn't like them."

Liz leaned forward. "Why not?"

"Because they used crude language that made me uncomfortable." She looked away. "And I think they did . . . things."

"What kind of things?" Liz asked.

Leah fiddled with a snag in her skirt. "I don't know. I didn't want to ask. But I told Gavin I did not approve, so he stopped taking me with him when he went out with friends." Her shoulders slumped and she went on in a quieter voice, "He went out a lot."

"Do you remember any of them? Any names he might have mentioned?"

"I'm sorry. I don't. For the last few months before I left Radcliff, we did not talk much."

The simple statement described such a miserable existence that pity for the poor girl nearly overpowered Liz. What a mess she'd gotten herself into when she left Pleasant Creek. Had Leah really wanted to leave the Amish?

Liz leaned forward. "Are you happy here?"

At first she didn't answer. Then she shrugged. "I have a job. A place to live. What more do I need?"

"Friends," Liz answered without hesitation. "And family."

Her eyes filled again. "I have no family," she whispered.

Then why did you ask about your Mutter and Vater when I arrived?

"That's not true. I've met your mother." Leah tried to withdraw her hands, but Liz held them tight. "Maybe if you contacted them—"

"No." She jerked her hands from Liz's. "They came to get me in Kentucky three times. The last time, my Vater told me I was no longer his daughter."

"I'm sure he didn't mean that."

"He did. He shouted at me. He was so angry he punched the wall and put a hole in it." Leah shuddered. "I never saw him like that before."

"He was upset. Maybe he'll change his mind. Especially if Viola talks to him."

Leah stood so abruptly the flimsy chair fell over behind her. "My Mutter would never go against him. He is her husband. But even if she did, Vater would not change his mind. You didn't see him that day." She shook her head. "I can never go back."

Thoughts whirled in Liz's brain. Surely there was *something* she could say to convince this poor child to go home. Even if she didn't want to return to the Amish, she would be a thousand times better off in Pleasant Creek than here. Someone would hire her to work in one of the town's businesses. She was about to say so when Leah dropped the wadded-up tissue into a garbage can and faced her.

"Thank you for coming to tell me about Gavin and Mrs. Younger. I must leave soon for work."

A clear dismissal. Liz stood and slung her purse over her shoulder.

"Do you mind if I give your address to the investigating police officers? Just in case they have more questions."

A pause, and then a slight nod.

She opened the door for Liz, who pulled a business card out of her purse and pressed it into Leah's hand as she exited.

"If there's anything I can ever do for you, please don't hesitate to call me."

As the door closed, Liz glimpsed tears sliding down the girl's face.

During the drive back to Pleasant Creek, a thought occurred to Liz. A memory of the steely faced man who accompanied the bishop to the inn rose in her mind. Asa Schwartz had been so angry with his daughter for running away with Gavin that he put his fist through a wall. Did he blame Gavin for luring Leah away?

And more importantly, had that anger cooled, or did it blaze strongly enough to commit murder?

Liz could not banish the mental image of Leah Schwartz's tears. That poor girl, living in a bare apartment with her books and nothing to offer guests except water and crackers. Was she correct in assuming her parents wouldn't welcome her home? Liz could hardly believe it. True, she didn't know Viola well, but she'd always seemed like a kind person. And yet, why had she not tried to convince Leah to return to Pleasant Creek instead of moving to Indianapolis?

But if Asa was still angry, maybe Leah was better off where she was.

It's none of my business. Her hands tightened on the steering wheel. *I should go down to Stan's office and tell him what I've learned.*

Even as the thought came to her, Liz knew she couldn't let the matter lie. That young woman deserved a better life.

The Schwartz farm lay on the southern outskirts of Pleasant Creek. Liz knew the location only vaguely, but after a few wrong turns she stumbled upon a mailbox with the name *Schwartz* painted in neat letters. The house was a white two-story with a steeply pitched roof. Along one side a line of laundry fluttered in the breeze; men's black broadfall trousers, homespun shirts, and plain dresses in sizes from adult down to children. Liz guided her car between the house and a pole barn. Before the Acura had rolled to a complete stop, a man exited the barn.

Her heart in her throat, Liz studied Asa Schwartz through the windshield. The only other time she'd seen him, she had not yet met Leah. Now the resemblance was obvious. The long, narrow face and hollow cheeks appeared more manly on him than on his daughter, but the shape was the same. Dark eyes stared at her from beneath a round-brimmed straw hat.

Were those the eyes of a killer?

Liz steeled herself and got out of the car. Relief flooded her when the door to the house opened and Viola appeared, a little girl at her side. She caught sight of Liz and a curious smile lit her features. She said something to the child, who nodded and disappeared inside as Viola descended the porch stairs.

"Liz, this is a surprise. Please come in. I have coffee and fresh zucchini bread."

The difference between this hospitable offering and the one she'd received in Indianapolis struck Liz as particularly sad, and she swallowed against a lump in her throat.

"Thank you, but I don't want to interrupt." She glanced at Asa, who had approached and stood silently. Liz forced a smile for him. "Hello."

While he did not smile, he regarded her with a pleasant expression, completely unlike the stony countenance he'd presented when he visited the inn. "Welcome to our home. A visit from a friend is always nice, and no interruption. Please come inside."

What a difference a few days had made in the man. What had happened to make him lose the tightfisted ire she'd witnessed before?

He gestured to the house. Liz paused only a moment before accepting the invitation. She stepped into a long living room, plenty big enough for a large family. It would easily house all the benches for an Amish church service when it was the Schwartzes' turn to act as host. Viola led her to the kitchen on her right, where the little girl Liz had spied earlier had already set out plates and coffee cups, and was placing a loaf of bread on the table. Liz smiled at the child as she slid into the chair Viola indicated.

Asa said something to the girl in Swiss, his tone soft. With a shy smile for Liz, she left the room.

While Viola poured coffee and cut thick slices of zucchini bread, Liz studied Asa out of the corner of her eye. He seemed like a typical Amish man, mild-mannered and pleasant. When Viola slid a plate in front of him, the gaze he turned up to her held unconcealed affection. Could a man like this hold a grudge long enough to commit murder? Now, seated in the Schwartz kitchen alongside him, Liz found that hard to believe.

But that wasn't the real reason for her visit.

When Viola had seated herself and Liz had expressed her appreciation for the delicious bread, an expectant hush fell over the couple.

Liz cleared her throat. "I have something to tell you, and I'm not sure how you'll feel about it."

"We heard about Gavin Younger." Viola glanced at her husband. "What a terrible tragedy."

The man's jaw tightened, and his lips formed a tight line. Ah, finally a glimpse of the dislike she'd seen before.

"Yes, it was, though I'm sure he wasn't one of your favorite people." Though she tried to keep any hint of accusation out of her comment, apparently she did not succeed.

Asa turned a surprised look her way. "Naturally he was not, but we would not wish him harm."

"Of course not," Liz hurried to say. "I didn't mean to imply you would." Though that was exactly what she'd intended.

"Gavin Younger has been in our prayers for more than a year," Viola said.

The comment caught Liz by surprise, even though it shouldn't have. "He has?"

"Ja." Asa cupped his mug in calloused hands and looked her directly in the eye. "If ever a young man needed the peace of Gött, it was him."

"Not only for that reason." Viola lowered her head, her gaze downcast. "We prayed that if he found Gött, perhaps he would bring our Leah home."

The two nodded, their expressions so transparent that Liz could not doubt their sincerity. She spoke softly. "Did you know that Leah and he were no longer together?"

"Not until three days ago." Viola pushed back her plate, the delicious bread untouched. "When Bishop Manz came with the news that Gavin was staying at your inn."

"The day I went with him to talk to you," Asa added.

Liz interrupted in a hurry. "I didn't know about Leah when I rented the room to him. If I had, I would have sent him away."

"Ja, you said so," Asa said. "I wanted to talk to him that day, to ask where our Leah is. But I waited too long." The man rubbed his eyes. "If only I had not hesitated."

"Why did you?"

His hand dropped, and he lifted a red-rimmed gaze to her face. "Because I needed to pray for self-control first. I did not want to accuse him or speak in anger."

Liz held his eyes for a long moment. The words were heartfelt, she was certain of it. This man genuinely desired to find his daughter, but he didn't want to risk losing his temper in the process. She'd glimpsed a bit of that anger and his struggle with self-control herself. The days he'd taken to pray had restored the sense of peace he sought, and the result was obvious. How could someone like that have committed murder?

She drew a breath. "Gavin isn't the reason I stopped by today." She glanced at Viola, and then fixed again on Asa's face. "I've just returned from a visit with Leah."

There was no mistaking the hope that sprang into the man's eyes. Viola leaped from her chair and rounded the table to stand at Liz's side.

"You've found her? Where is she? Is she well?"

The questions resolved any lingering doubt about Leah's welcome, should she decide to return. And if Liz was any judge at all, the young woman deeply desired to.

"She is well," Liz told them, "but I don't think she's happy. She is living alone in Indianapolis."

"Indianapolis. That is why our letters to Radcliff were sent back."

Asa stood, his hands planted on the surface of the table. "Please give us the address. We will hire a car and go to her today."

Liz's first inclination was to offer to drive them herself, but she'd already been gone for hours. With everything going on at the inn, she needed to get back. Instead, she let them borrow her phone to call a driver. She gave them the note with Leah's address, and also told them about her job at the grocery store in case she wasn't at home. When she left, the couple were readying themselves for the trip to Indianapolis.

Stan would still need to be told everything she'd discovered today, but she felt confident Asa Schwartz was in no danger of being accused of Gavin's murder.

17

Liz parked her car in the garage and then took a walk around the outside of the four-season room. Where had the Three Eagles made their escape? She found the evidence on the far side of the house. A once-beautiful mound of yellow mums had been ruined, the ravished blossoms crushed by three heavy pairs of shoes. The gutter looked okay, so apparently the Three Eagles had managed to jump down from the porch roof without dislodging it. If the only damage was to a perennial that would return next year, she could count herself fortunate.

The back door opened when she approached, and Sarah stood in the entrance.

"Hello," Liz said. "Thanks for covering for me this morning."

"Of course." She looked miserable. "Gavin's dead? I can't believe it."

"It was quite a shock." Liz forced herself not to look in the direction of the gazebo.

The young woman glanced over her shoulder into the house and stepped outside, pulling the door closed behind her. Troubled lines creased the smooth forehead beneath her Kapp.

"Is everything okay?" Liz asked.

She glanced again over her shoulder. "I have something to tell you."

What would cause sweet Sarah to look so guilty? Had she broken something valuable? "Okay," Liz said. "Go on."

"I know where Caleb Porter is."

The confession came from out of the blue and surprised Liz so that for a moment she couldn't speak. Finally, she said, "Where is he? We have to tell his parents. They've been worried sick."

Sarah raised her other hand to her cheek, her face flooded with guilt. "I did not know that until this morning when I arrived. Isaac went immediately to get Caleb and bring him here."

"Wait. Caleb is here?"

She nodded. "But his parents do not know. No one does."

"Why hasn't he told his parents he's okay?" Liz tilted her head and studied the girl. Though she would stake her career on the fact that Sarah hadn't a dishonest bone in her body, her obvious guilt didn't bode well. "Where has he been, anyway?"

"Hiding in Anna Beachy's barn."

Sorrow stabbed at Liz so sharply she could have cried. So Caleb *was* involved in Gavin's murder. That nice young man had somehow gotten pulled into a circle of dishonesty, one that Liz had inadvertently created when she rented a room to Gavin Younger. And then he'd gone into hiding.

"You'd better take me to him," she told Sarah.

When Liz entered the four-season room, she was surprised to find not only Caleb, but also Sarah's husband, Isaac, Anna, and a middle-aged Amish man she didn't know. The men rose from their seats when they caught sight of her. Caleb glanced at her once and then hung his head. Liz paused, considering how to react. Finally she crossed the room and came to a stop before the stranger.

"I don't believe we've met. I'm Liz Eckardt."

"Aden Beachy." He bobbed his head. "I am Vater to Anna."

"So Caleb has been in hiding at your house."

"Not at my house," Aden corrected. "In my barn. Anna did not tell me or my wife of his presence."

Liz glanced toward Anna, who failed to meet her gaze. "But why would you—" She snapped her mouth shut on the question. "Before we say another word, we need to get Eunice and Otis." She ducked her head and forced Caleb to meet her eye. "They have looked everywhere for you, and so have the police."

He opened his mouth as if to speak, but then closed it again. With a look of resignation, he nodded.

"I will get them." Sarah hurried from the room.

Liz called after her, "While you're there, ask the officer in the rotunda to call Stan Houghton. He needs to know about this."

An awkward silence settled in the room after she'd gone. Questions crowded Liz's mind, but she forced herself to hold them until the Porters arrived. Thankfully, only a few minutes passed before the worried parents burst into the room. Eunice threw herself into Caleb's arms, sobbing, while Otis encircled them both in a tight embrace. Sarah also returned and went to stand beside her husband. Liz glanced at Anna, who watched the reunion with a look of pure misery on her face. Had the girl not thought about what Caleb's parents must have felt while she hid him away?

But the bigger question pressed forward in Liz's mind—why was he in hiding?

Officer Hughes appeared, looking stern and official. "Chief says I'm to make sure no one leaves until he gets here. He's coming right over."

Caleb untangled himself from his parents. "Don't worry. I'm not going anywhere." His shoulders lifted as he drew in a deep breath and looked down into his mother's face. "Not ever."

"What?" Eunice gave her head a vicious shake. "I don't understand."

Neither did Liz, but obviously the explanation would take some time.

"Why don't we sit down while we sort this out?" she said.

Everyone took a seat—except Hughes, who hovered in the doorway and glowered around the room. Though Stan would need to hear any explanations, Caleb was not inclined to wait.

"Mother, Dad, I have something important to tell you." His gaze strayed to Anna, who gave him an encouraging nod. "I'm not going home with you."

"What are you talking about?" Eunice put a hand up to his forehead. "Are you coming down with a fever?"

Caleb took her hand and cradled it gently between his. "I'm not sick. I've given this a lot of thought, and I've decided to become Amish."

"Don't be ridiculous, son," Otis said. "We're Baptists."

Caleb answered with a smile in his father's direction. "I've learned a lot about the Amish over the past couple of days. Their faith is not just a set of beliefs." His voice took on an ardent note. "It's a way of living peacefully with God. It's all about separating yourself from anything that distracts you and dedicating yourself to Him."

The reason for his absence became clear to Liz. She looked at Anna. "So while Caleb has been hiding in your barn, you've been telling him about your faith."

"I have been answering his questions." She raised her chin. "He showed up at our house with a bag of napoleons from Sweet Everything as a gift, in return for answers. How could I refuse?"

A deep-red flush crept over Eunice's face. "You're confused, Caleb. I insist that you stop talking nonsense this instant."

The look he gave her held a touch of compassion. "Mother, I've never been more certain about anything in my life. I've been studying the Amish lifestyle for months, ever since we started planning this trip. Once I got here and I saw their dedication, and how *real* they are, I knew I wanted that lifestyle for myself."

Though he had remained silent, Anna's father spoke up now. "If the young man is serious, our community will welcome him."

Eunice's lips pursed. "I won't have it." She turned sideways in her chair to face her son. "You're coming home with us, and that's final."

"I knew you'd react this way. That's why I snuck away. I needed time to think on my own, without you telling me what to do." His mouth hardened into the same expression as his mother's, though he was probably unaware of it. "Telling me what to *think*."

Obviously this was a conversation that needed to take place in private. Still, Liz couldn't stop herself from asking a question.

"Caleb, did you see Gavin Younger before you left?"

Out of the corner of her eye she saw Officer Hughes stiffen to attention.

The young man shook his head, looking uneasy for the first time. "I didn't. I know it looks bad, but I promise I didn't even know about his death until Isaac came to get me."

Liz believed him. Her fears concerning Caleb's involvement in the murder alleviated, Liz felt an urgent need to escape the tension of this room. Let Stan sort through the mess.

She stood. "If you'll excuse me, I have some things to attend to."

In the kitchen, she came upon Beans lapping water from his bowl. Bending to scratch behind his ear, she asked, "How are you doing, boy?"

The dog responded by half-closing his eyes and leaning into her leg. Apparently her talk with Betty had worked, and Frank was being kept out of Beans's hair. Or fur. His attitude seemed almost normal. She finished with a pat on his back and then headed for her quarters. Beans followed her a few steps, then headed for the front of the house, presumably to take up his usual post in the foyer.

In the act of unlocking the door to her quarters, Liz happened to be watching the dog when he stepped through the doorway. A streak of black and white leaped from the shadows, bounced off his head, and came to a graceful landing on the ornamental rug. With a frightened yelp, Beans's hind legs scrabbled on the hardwood for a second before he found traction and scampered away.

"You did that on purpose, you sneaky thing." Liz stomped across the kitchen and snatched up the cat, who was calmly cleaning a paw.

"Meow," came the sweet reply.

Betty's heels clacked on the hardwood floor, alerting Liz to her approach.

"There you are." She lifted Frank from Liz's arms and continued speaking in a baby-talk voice. "We're going for a ride in the car. Won't that be nice?"

Tempted to mention the cat's clandestine attack on poor Beans, instead Liz focused on the woman's words. "Oh, are you checking out?" With an effort, she filtered a hopeful tone out of her voice.

"The moment Chief Houghton gives me permission," came the reply. "In the meantime, he did say we weren't confined here, didn't he?"

"He did."

"Then we're going for a ride in the country." She hugged Frank close. "I hope a change of scenery will calm my poor abused nerves."

Calm your *abused nerves?* Liz replied with a pleasant, "Have a nice drive."

"Good news," Mary Ann announced when Liz entered Sew Welcome a bit later. "Insurance will cover the rug, the hardwood floors, and damaged merchandise, and will even replace the locks."

"That's great." Liz made a wide circle around the paint-stained carpet and collapsed onto a stool at the back counter. She propped her elbows on the surface and dropped her chin onto her hands. "I'm glad something is going right."

Mary Ann slid a bolt of fabric into place on the shelves and turned to peer at her. "The stress is beginning to tell on you, isn't it?"

"I'm okay. But I'd be better if I could get a good night's sleep."

As if to prove the point, she gave a huge yawn.

"I have just the thing." Mary Ann crossed to the small refrigerator in the corner. She removed a pie with a high, fluffy white dome. "It's coconut cream."

Liz grinned. "I feel better already." She looked around the room. "Where is Sadie? Coconut cream is her favorite."

Mary Ann removed paper plates and a knife from beneath the counter. "She a bit under the weather today. Headache. I expect the paint fumes are the cause."

"I can certainly understand that," Liz said. "I hope she's okay."

"I'm sure she'll be fine. I'll take her a slice of pie later." She grinned. "If we have any left, that is."

The first delicious bite improved Liz's mood considerably.

"Oh!" She straightened on the stool. "I ran an errand this morning."

As they enjoyed the pie, Liz recounted her visit with Leah and the subsequent conversation with Asa and Viola.

"I pray that girl comes to her senses." Mary Ann shook her head. "She belongs with her family and friends, not stuck in a lonely apartment far from home."

They were finishing their snack when Betty entered the shop, Frank clutched to her chest.

"That was a short drive," Liz commented as the woman hurried over to them.

"Oh my goodness." The woman dropped into a chair and began to fan her face with a pair of gloves. "Oh my dears, I can't believe it. I *don't* believe it."

Her cheeks were flushed, and her breath came in shallow pants. Liz and Mary Ann exchanged a concerned glance.

"Are you all right?" Liz asked. "Can I get you a glass of water or a cup of tea?"

"No." The gloves flapped in Liz's direction. "Give me a moment. I need to think."

Liz's concern deepened when Betty began to rock back and forth in the stationary chair, mumbling, "It can't be. But evidence doesn't lie."

She left her stool and went to Betty's side. Placing a hand on her arm, she spoke in a calming tone. "Something has obviously upset you. Can you tell us what it is?"

"I suppose I must. Something like this can't remain a secret, can it?"

"We don't know," Mary Ann replied in a steady voice. "But if you'll tell us we'll try to help."

Betty nodded. "Yes, I suppose I must. Come with me. I'll show you."

She leaped out of the chair and Frank dropped to the floor. Liz and Mary Ann followed her out of Sew Welcome—Liz taking care to shut the shop's door to keep the cat away from Beans—and out of the inn. Betty's car, a black Buick Century, was parked out front at the curb, and she halted by the rear bumper.

"I went out for a calming drive, as you know." She looked at Liz, who nodded. "I decided to visit my brother at the cabin and bring him up to date on everything that has happened here. He declined my offer of dinner last night and hasn't answered my calls this morning."

In light of recent events, Liz's mind leaped to an unpleasant conclusion. "I hope he's okay."

"So do I." Worry choked Betty's voice. "He's not himself lately, what with being unemployed. Not himself at all."

She said the last in such a plaintive tone that Liz instinctively spoke to reassure her. "You two must be very close."

Tears sprang into Betty's eyes. "We're really not. He's so busy he rarely has time for me. So, naturally, when he asked me to come here I leaped at the opportunity."

Her voice wavered on the last word. Liz had never heard the proud woman sound so uncertain. Something had happened to shake her deeply.

"Maybe we should call Stan and ask him to send someone out to the cabin to check on your brother."

Betty's chin trembled. "Yes, I'm sure we should call the police. But first let me show you what I found."

"In the woods?" Mary Ann asked.

"That's right. I knocked on the cabin door, but Benjamin refused to let me in. He said he was busy and would call me later, so I returned to my car. But when I opened the door, Frank leaped out. He ran off into the woods and would not return when I called him." A hand fluttered at her collarbone. "My dears, I was distraught. What if a wild animal got him? So I followed, calling after him. He led me on a chase through the wild, the naughty boy. Just look at this."

She extended a leg to display her slacks covered in burrs. Liz judged it wise to hold her tongue about the "naughty boy."

"And then he circled back toward the car. I caught him when he sat down to wash his paws. We came up on the cabin from behind, and I was so relieved I almost missed it. But there it was, right outside Benjamin's back door."

Liz glanced at Mary Ann. "It?"

Betty nodded. "I didn't see it before it went missing, but I . . . overheard you talking about it. I hope I'm wrong, I really do. Maybe this isn't the right one. But—" Her lip clutched between her teeth, she pressed a button on her key fob. The lock on the Buick released, and the trunk popped open.

Inside was the lamp Liz had bought at Louise Younger's estate auction. It had been destroyed.

18

When he arrived, the chief stared down at the lamp in the trunk of Betty's car. "You're sure it's the same one?"

"I'm sure," Liz verified. "I'd never seen an alabaster base with marbling like that. It's one reason I wanted the lamp."

The beautiful base had been broken and lay in two pieces, still connected inside by wiring. Also in the trunk lay the creamy-yellow shade, which had been flattened as though stomped with a boot.

Stan snapped a few pictures with his cell phone, then gave Betty a stern stare as he pulled on a pair of gloves. "I wish you'd called me before you picked it up."

The poor woman wrung her hands, tears obviously near the surface. "I should have. At the time I couldn't think straight. I was afraid this would implicate Benjamin in the theft or—" She gulped. "Worse. My first instinct was to protect my little brother."

Mary Ann placed an arm around the woman's shoulders and squeezed, while Stan mumbled something that sounded like "tampering with evidence." Then he lifted the fragments from the trunk. Now that she got a better look, Liz saw that the base had not been broken. The two pieces screwed together. The bottom part looked heavy, while the alabaster top—which was shaped like a squatty, curved vase—was hollow.

Stan held it in front of his nose and peered inside. "Looks like there are a few threads stuck on the edges. See there?"

With one rubber-gloved finger he pointed. Liz, Mary Ann, and Betty all bent close to examine scraps of white fabric clinging to the roughened edges of the rusty metal fitting.

"Something *was* hidden inside." Liz looked up at Mary Ann, triumphant. "We were right. We just looked in the wrong item."

"But what would fit in that space?" Betty asked.

The opening was only about two and a half inches in diameter.

"Money, maybe." Stan tilted the lamp and shone the light on his cell phone up inside. "Looks like a handy place to stash some cash."

"Or jewelry," Mary Ann suggested. "I don't know if Louise had any pieces of value, but if so, she might have wanted to keep them hidden."

A patrol car pulled up to the curb behind them and Officer Dixon emerged.

Stan replaced the broken lamp in the trunk and turned to him. "Glad you're here. Get an evidence kit and bag this. Put a rush on the prints, just like the others. I want someone to run it over to the lab personally."

"Will do."

"Then you and George go out to the Lakeside Cabins, number—" He raised his eyebrows and looked at Betty.

"Six," she supplied miserably. "Please don't tell him I turned him in. This whole thing is just so upsetting."

"We'll protect your identity, ma'am." Stan turned back to Dixon. "Cabin number six. Pick up Benjamin Baggett and take him to headquarters. I'll be along shortly to question him."

Betty sniffled as they all stepped up on the sidewalk. The officer began his work in the trunk of her car.

"You got my message?" Liz asked the chief, who nodded. "Caleb and the others are out in the four-season room."

Betty turned to her. "Caleb has been found? How relieved his parents must be."

"Well . . ." The whole story was far too complicated to go into now. "Yes. They are relieved to know where he is."

Stan turned on his heel, and then snapped his fingers and stopped. "I almost forgot. Guess who the state police picked up just this side of the Allen County line?"

Liz offered a guess. "The Three Eagles?"

"Bingo. They're bringing them back here for questioning." He switched his gaze to Betty. "Thank you for cooperating with us, ma'am. You're free to leave whenever you want."

"Oh." The woman glanced back at her car, her expression lost. "I-I'm not quite sure."

How funny that an hour ago she'd been so vocal about her desire to leave. Still, Liz understood. She'd just implicated her own brother in a murder investigation. Naturally she would want be nearby while he was questioned.

"You're welcome to stay a few days," Liz told her without thinking. She flinched inwardly. How could she ever face Beans when she'd just extended his tormentor's stay?

A grateful sigh seeped from Betty's lips. "Thank you."

Stan continued. "I'm going to assign extra patrols in this area to be on the safe side, but I don't see any reason to keep a pair of officers here since we've got the suspects in custody." His lips widened into a grin. "I know Three Eagles who are about to have their wings clipped."

He headed for the inn, chuckling at his own joke.

She and the others watched Dixon put the lamp in a plastic evidence bag. When he left, they returned to the inn and settled in the sitting room. Though she would have loved to hear Stan question Caleb and the others, she hated to intrude on the Porters' family struggles.

Betty accepted a cup of coffee—full strength this time, with lots of cream—and collapsed into a chair. "My poor nerves can't take much more."

"I know what you mean." Liz settled on the sofa with Mary Ann beside her. "This has certainly been a stressful few days."

"Theft. Murder." Betty shuddered. "And my dear brother somehow involved. I can't believe Benjamin is capable of murder. In fact, I don't believe it."

Mary Ann sipped from her cup and set it on a coaster. "Was your brother acquainted with Gavin?"

"I don't see how. Benjamin has never lived in Indiana. We were born in Frankfort, Kentucky, where I still live." A smile played about her lips, and her eyes became unfocused with a memory. "He was always a dreamer. Always had a grand scheme for becoming wealthy. 'This is how I'm going to make my first million, sis,' he'd tell me." She exhaled a long, slow breath. "But his ideas never paid off. He worked in retail for a while, and then he got a good job at a distillery in Frankfort. But there was a bit of trouble over some valuable memorabilia that went missing, and he left there."

Liz caught Mary Ann's eye. If she were to hazard a guess, the missing memorabilia had probably ended up in Benjamin's possession.

Betty absently stirred her coffee. "He stayed with me for a while, but then found work at another distillery about ninety miles southwest of Frankfort."

"Oh?" Mary Ann asked. "Where was that?"

"The distillery isn't well known. It's located in a small town called Radcliff."

In the midst of taking a sip of coffee, Liz nearly choked. She set the cup down with a clatter. "Radcliff? But that's where Gavin lived."

Mary Ann had gone pale. "The last time I spoke with Louise, I asked after Gavin. She said he'd taken a job at a distillery in Kentucky."

Thoughts whirled like a cyclone in Liz's mind. Obviously the two men had known each other. What were the odds that Gavin and

Benjamin, employees of the same distillery, would end up at the same time in Pleasant Creek, hundreds of miles from home? That could not be a coincidence. They must have arranged to meet here.

But why?

"Gavin wanted whatever Louise stored in that lamp." Mary Ann's words came slowly, as if she were reasoning them out as she spoke. "What if he told Benjamin about it, and Benjamin came up here to steal it from Gavin?"

"Oh!" Tears filled Betty's eyes. "I can't believe it of my brother."

Liz leaned forward, her arms planted on her knees. "How did you find out about the Olde Mansion Inn, Betty? Didn't you say your brother told you?"

"Y-yes. He'd quit his job and was coming here to relax before finding another one. He wanted to spend time with me, but knew I would not be comfortable in a rustic cabin, so he suggested I call you."

A horrible idea occurred to Liz. "How long did you have my number before you called?"

"No time at all. Benjamin told me this was a busy inn and suggested I call immediately. I was grateful you had an opening on such short notice."

Liz's stomach soured. The wedding party had canceled just that morning because of the hit-and-run accident that had injured the groom the night before. How had Benjamin known she would have an opening? He couldn't, unless he also knew about the wedding party's cancelation.

And the accident.

She stood. "We need Stan."

"Then it's a good thing I'm already here." Pleasant Creek's police chief strode into the room, arms swinging easily at his side. His posture was far more relaxed than it had been half an hour before. Apparently the conversation with Caleb and the others had gone well.

Liz lowered herself back onto the couch and indicated that he should take a seat. "I think we're on to something you'll want to know."

Speaking quickly, she brought him up to speed. His relaxed expression gradually became serious, and the telling tic in his cheek began to twitch.

"No," Betty insisted when Liz came to the part about the wedding party. "I can't believe that of my brother. Benjamin would not run down a bicycler any more than he would stab that young man. It had to be someone else."

Mary Ann smoothed a silver strand of hair behind her ear. "I tend to agree. And why would he involve his sister?"

Stan answered without hesitation. "To have an excuse to come to the Olde Mansion Inn. He did come here, didn't he?" He asked the question of Liz, who nodded.

"For coffee hour. But Gavin wasn't here," she pointed out. "In fact, Gavin didn't have a reservation at all. He simply showed up. And yet . . ." Liz spoke slowly, possibilities crowding into her mind. "Maddox called the same day."

"Ah." Stan leaned back in his chair. "We're back to the mysterious singers who aren't really singers."

Liz sat up. "They're not?"

Of course they weren't. How foolish she had been. She'd even suspected the ruse herself, but had fallen for Phil's explanation like a gullible schoolgirl.

Stan pulled out his cell phone and held his thumbs in readiness over the screen. "What did Maddox say when he called? Be as specific as you can."

Liz thought back. "He said they saw my website and wondered if I had any rooms. That they'd been on the road for a few days singing for various benefits and needed a break because their tenor's throat was getting scratchy."

"Baritone," Betty corrected. "Phil, the baritone, is the one with the sore throat. Donnie is the tenor."

At coffee hour when Betty met the trio she had bragged about her musical experience. Liz remembered her pointing out each member of the trio. Maddox the bass, Phil the baritone, and Donnie the tenor. She sank against the back cushion. Why hadn't she caught the slip then?

"Maddox told me on the phone their *tenor* had a scratchy throat," she told Stan.

"He also told you his name was Maddox."

She blinked. "It's not?"

Stan shook his head. "Real name's Kurt Mardel. The other two are Andrew Plummer and Ed Collins. The lab ID'd them from the prints we lifted in their rooms."

She struggled to process that information. "If you were able to identify their fingerprints so quickly, does that mean they have a criminal record?"

"Nope. Clean as mine. They're government contractors. Mardel is a security systems expert, Collins a communications specialist, and Plummer's a security guard. They all have spotless records and high military clearance. I verified it with the feds and the Kentucky State Police."

Liz grasped her head and pressed her hands against her skull, as if that would clear the chaos in her mind. "It doesn't make sense. Why would people like that pretend to be a singing group and want to stay at the inn?"

"That's one of the questions I intend to ask them while they're guests at my jail." Stan's smile held an icy chill.

"Wait a minute." Mary Ann's eyes narrowed. "You said you contacted the *Kentucky* authorities?"

The grin that spread across the chief's face this time was genuine. He pointed at the older woman. "Good catch. Take a guess where that group lives."

Liz pictured the registration sheet Maddox—or Kurt Mardel—filled out. "It isn't Cincinnati, is it?" He didn't even have to shake his head. She already knew. "They're from Radcliff, aren't they?"

"Two are. Collins lives nearby, in—"

"Fort Knox!" Mary Ann's shout, which was out of character for the normally calm woman, startled everyone. She leaped from her chair. "I know what's going on. Wait here."

She ran from the room.

Details began clicking into place. Liz turned toward Stan, who nodded.

"Radcliff is just over five miles from Fort Knox. That's how I knew they were somehow connected to Younger."

"And to Benjamin." Betty sniffled.

They heard the door to Sew Welcome open and moments later Mary Ann returned carrying a newspaper. And Frank.

"I was afraid we might have thrown it away during the cleanup." She clutched the newspaper as she crossed the room and deposited the cat into Betty's lap. "By the way, you owe me for several yards of houndstooth wool. He seems to favor that for sharpening his claws."

While Betty scolded the "naughty boy" in an indulgent tone, Mary Ann handed the newspaper to Stan.

"We read about it last week," she explained. "Someone robbed Fort Knox. The paper said the theft would have taken several people to accomplish."

Liz held up three fingers and ticked them off one at a time. "How about a security guard, a communications specialist, and a security systems expert?"

Stan studied the article. Rising, he mumbled something about making a call and left the room.

Mary Ann returned to her seat, her expression troubled. "I can see how those three could accomplish a theft, but what did they steal? And what's even more puzzling is how men with high security clearance could be involved with a pair of distillery workers." She bit her lower lip and glanced at Betty. "I don't mean to be a snob, but it's unlikely they'd run in the same circles."

"Wait." Liz hopped out of her chair and paced to the fireplace, thinking hard. "That's one thing that *does* make sense. Like you said the other day, Fort Knox doesn't keep just gold bricks anymore. Whatever those three stole, it must have been worth a lot of money to make them risk their careers. But what would they do with it after they'd stolen it? Would three men with reputable jobs know how to contact people who would buy stolen property?"

Mary Ann picked up the train of thought. "They'd have to contact someone who could handle the sale for them. Someone like Gavin and—" She offered Betty an apologetic grimace. "Benjamin."

Betty hugged Frank to her chest, sniffling. "Oh my poor nerves."

"Gavin was in jail for possession of stolen merchandise," Liz said. "But it was a watch. Nothing that could have come from Fort Knox."

Mary Ann shook her head. "It would have to be something that would bring a big enough price for those three to risk their careers."

"Agreed. But what?" Liz laid an arm across the mantel and drummed her fingers.

Betty ventured a guess. "Something small enough to fit inside a lamp?"

19

Liz widened her eyes. "That must be it. The Three Eagles, or whoever they are, stole something worth a lot of money. Jewelry, maybe. And they gave it to Gavin to sell. Maybe it was going to take a while to make the right contacts, so Gavin had to hide the stuff somewhere. He paid a visit to his aunt—"

"On the pretext of painting her house," Mary Ann put in.

Another piece of the puzzle. "Right," Liz said. "He shoved the loot in the lamp, which he would have known was hollow since it was in his room when he lived there. But then he got arrested and went to jail. And while he was there, the three found a buyer themselves. So they went to Fort Wayne to find the stuff, and while they were going through the house, Louise came home."

Sorrow crept over Mary Ann's features. "They stabbed her."

The only problem with that scenario was that Liz couldn't envision any of the Three Eagles killing an elderly lady. But Benjamin? She stole a surreptitious glance at Betty, who stroked Frank with such nervous movements she almost felt sorry for the cat.

"Gavin must not have told them where he hid whatever it was," Mary Ann said, "otherwise they would have taken the lamp then."

"Of course not. Gavin wouldn't have told them. Otherwise they could do exactly as they did—cut him out of the deal."

Liz closed her eyes, trying to connect all the unusual occurrences since Gavin's arrival at the inn. The Three Eagles deciding to go to the auction made sense. They probably knew when Gavin would get out of jail and hoped he would be there. They planned to connect with him after he bought the lamp. Only their plan went astray when Gavin was late and *she* bought the lamp instead.

But they'd arrived at the inn *before* she bought the lamp.

"I suppose Gavin intended to connect with them here, in Pleasant Creek, to turn over the stolen items."

"That makes sense." Mary Ann shook her head. "This was Gavin's home for several years. He probably knew every road in the county, and every tree in every patch of woods. He could easily arrange a clandestine meeting here."

"But why the Olde Mansion Inn? How could he have known I'd have vacancies?"

Betty piped up in a mournful tone. "He couldn't if he was in jail. But Benjamin could, if he . . ." her eyelids fluttered closed, and her voiced dropped to a whisper, "arranged that bicycle accident."

Stan strode back into the room then, his cell phone clutched in his hand. "You were right," he told Mary Ann. "Those three are under suspicion for the theft at Fort Knox."

"What did they steal?" Liz asked.

"The FBI agent wouldn't say. Just told me to hold them and they'd send someone shortly to pick them up. But I intend to question them first. I hate dealing with the feds." He shoved the phone in his pocket, then looked up at Betty. "Got another call. Dixon and Hughes didn't pick up your brother."

Hope sprang into her face. "He convinced them he is not involved?"

"Nope. The cabin was empty. Appears he left in a hurry." Stan frowned. "Looks like another bird has flown the coop."

Caleb agreed to stay the night at the inn, though from the firm set of his jaw Liz sensed that his determination to follow through with his plan to join the Amish would not be shaken. She wished all three Porters good night and spared a sympathetic thought for poor Eunice, who looked like her world had been shattered. Betty also retired early, clutching Frank and looking nearly as downcast as Eunice.

In her quarters, Liz ate a supper of tomato soup and a ham sandwich while the television played a sitcom she usually found amusing. Tonight she couldn't focus. The events of the day continued to occupy her thoughts to the point of distraction. She was so tired her body felt as though weights had been attached to her limbs, but she doubted sleep would find her tonight.

The next thing she knew, the ringtone on her cell phone pulled her out of a deep slumber. Groggy and stiff, she stretched out on the sofa and arched her aching back. What time was it? She glanced at the clock, blinking to see clearly. Eleven forty. Five forty in Kosovo. Steve had mentioned last night he was working odd hours.

It took her a few moments to find her phone, and it continued to ring as she fished it out from the crack between the couch cushions. A glance at the screen revealed the caller was not Steve.

"Mary Ann?" she said through a yawn. "Is everything okay?"

"I don't know!" An unconcealed note of panic rang in her friend's voice. "Something dreadful must have happened."

Liz's pulse kicked up a notch. "What?"

She minimized the call to reveal an incoming text. A single word, sent from Sadie's cell phone.

HELP!

She slapped the phone to her ear. "Should we call an ambulance?"

"I was thinking maybe we should call Stan instead."

Panic erupted in her chest. With everything that had happened lately, Stan was the only choice. She leaped off the sofa.

"I'll call him," she nearly shouted into the phone. "Are you driving, or am I?"

"I'll be right there."

The call clicked off. With trembling fingers she punched in Stan's number. He answered with a groggy, "'Lo?"

"Sadie is in trouble." While she searched for the shoes she'd kicked off, she explained about the text.

He sounded instantly alert. "It's probably nothing. Maybe she fell or something. I'll send a car out there. You stay put, do you hear me?"

Like *that* was likely when her friend needed help. Without answering she disconnected the call, snatched up her purse, and ran from the room.

Beans raised his head to stare at her when she raced out the front door. As she shut and locked the door behind her, Mary Ann's car pulled up to the curb. Liz hopped into the passenger seat.

"Stan is sending someone," she told her friend. "He told me to stay put."

"You'd think he'd know us better than that," Mary Ann said as she veered onto the street.

"I'm still wondering if we should call an ambulance too?"

Mary Ann continued to watch the road, but shook her head. "I tried to call her as soon as I got the text. She's turned her phone off."

Which meant she didn't want an incoming call. Because of the noise?

"What if it's . . .?" Liz hated to voice the name.

"Benjamin Baggett?" Mary Ann suggested. "I thought the same."

Liz's stomach twisted. "Hurry."

The drive to the Schwarzentruber farm seemed to take forever, though it was only a few miles out of town. Long before they approached the big white house, Mary Ann turned off her headlights. A bright full moon cast its white light all around, but Liz hoped the lack of headlights would at least partially hide their approach. When Sadie's house came into view, Mary Ann pulled the car off the road and cut the engine.

"Maybe we'd better go the rest of the way on foot." Though her voice sounded completely calm, the taut cords in Mary Ann's slender neck stood out visibly. "Just in case."

Her throat so tight she could barely breathe, Liz managed to squeak, "Agreed."

The pair exited the car, taking care to make no noise when they shut the doors. Cold night air chilled Liz in an instant. Sensible Mary Ann had grabbed a jacket.

They approached the dark house from the side, mindful that if Benjamin was inside with Sadie, he might be watching the front. He wouldn't hurt an elderly lady, would he? An answering thought snatched the breath from her chest. Louise Younger had been an elderly lady, and it hadn't stopped her from being stabbed in her own home. Liz quickened her pace.

By unspoken agreement, they circled to the back. The house loomed over them. Anyone might be watching through the three dark windows on the second floor. Chills from more than cold rose along the flesh on Liz's arms.

They reached the back door, and her heart sank to her feet. The screen dangled loose, the edges sliced from the frame, and the inside door stood ajar. Mary Ann lifted a hand to cover her mouth, fear apparent in her eyes.

We should wait for Stan, Liz mouthed without making a sound.

The two stared at each other a moment, and then as one, approached the door. Sadie had cried out for help. They couldn't wait.

Liz pulled her sleeve down over her hand so she wouldn't disturb any fingerprints, and gently pressed down on the handle. The screen door squeaked as it swung open, the sound ripping through the silence of the night like a scream. Swallowing against a desert-dry mouth, Liz stepped in front of Mary Ann and entered first. If Benjamin waited on the other side, he'd attack her before her friend.

She pushed the inside door open. The hinges moved noiselessly, thank goodness. Stepping as lightly as she could, she entered Sadie's spacious kitchen, Mary Ann close on her heels. A quick glance around showed nothing out of place.

Mary Ann pointed toward the hallway, and Liz nodded. Sadie's bedroom lay in that direction, on the first floor. They crept forward, every creak of the old hardwood magnified in their ears. Liz strained to hear any other sound in the silent house.

The door to Sadie's bedroom stood open. Drawing comfort from Mary Ann's hand on her back, Liz leaned through the doorway and glanced around the room. Only when she was certain nobody was hiding around the corner did she enter.

The room was empty.

"She's not here," Mary Ann whispered, nodding toward the bed.

The quilt had been thrown back, and an indentation in the pillow indicated Sadie had lain there recently.

A wave of nausea gripped Liz. "She's been kidnapped."

Mary Ann said, "Either that, or—"

A gunshot split the night's silence.

"That came from outside." Liz's whisper sounded like a shout.

The two dashed from the room. Every bit of logic in Liz's mind shouted, *Wait for the police!* But how could she? Anything could be happening to her friend right now.

They exited the house at a run and turned to the right. The location of the shot was obvious. Screams rang in the darkness, high-pitched and fueled by agony. Liz pulled ahead of Mary Ann in her dash toward the toolshed. From the corner of her eye she caught sight of another running figure moments before they nearly collided. Terror shot through her when a strong arm snatched her off her feet and a hand clamped over her mouth.

20

"I told you to stay home." Stan's furious whisper sounded in her ear.

All strength left Liz's knees and she would have fallen had his arm not held her up. She allowed herself to be ushered to the corner of the building, where Mary Ann stood. Stan released Liz and motioned for the two of them to stay put. His revolver in hand, he doubled back toward the entrance.

The screams became discernable words. "You shot me! I can't believe you shot me, you crazy old bat!"

"Oh hush. You deserve it. You were going to stab me." Relief zipped through Liz when she heard Sadie's irascible voice. "Besides, any thief stupid enough to let me put on my housecoat and sneak my gun out of the bedside table deserves to be shot. You're not a very smart criminal, you know."

"For heaven's sake, Sadie," Stan said, his tone lightly scolding. "Do you know how much paperwork I'll have to fill out to explain this?"

Mary Ann and Liz collapsed in each other's arms, laughter that held a ring of hysteria rising from their throats. Elbows locked, they rounded the corner and entered the barn. There they found Sadie standing over Benjamin, who writhed before her on the dirt floor. In her hand she held the revolver she kept in her nightstand, the business end pointed at his head. Moonlight filtered through the open doorway and illuminated a pool of thick white liquid on the ground. Liz identified the substance at once from the odor. Paint.

Stan stepped around the puddle and kicked a wicked-looking knife out of the moaning man's reach. Then he pulled a penlight out of his pocket and shone it on the wound, a bleeding gash in his thigh.

"You'll be all right," he told Benjamin. "It's just a flesh wound. She didn't hit the bone or the artery."

"I wasn't aiming for the bone," Sadie said. "If I had been, I would have hit it."

She sounded her usual cocky self, but Liz detected a bit of tension in her voice. She and Mary Ann went to wrap her in a hug.

"I'm glad you're okay," Liz said.

The smile she awarded them trembled only slightly. "Thanks for coming to my rescue."

"You obviously didn't need us." Mary Ann waved toward Benjamin. "You had things well in hand, as usual."

"Look in his pocket," Sadie told Stan. "He got something out of the paint can, but wouldn't show me. I'm dying to know what it is."

Mary Ann shuddered. "Don't say that, even jokingly."

There was no mistaking which pocket the man had stashed the item in. The right side of his jacket was covered in paint.

"Go ahead, Baggett," Stan ordered. "Hand it over."

The man produced a sticky packet and, with a sneer, tossed it at Stan's feet.

"All right." Stan didn't move, nor did the hard stare he fixed on the man waver. "Now the rest of it."

Benjamin set his jaw in a stubborn pose. "I don't know what you're talking about."

"Whatever you got out of the lamp." The police chief's steady glare did not waver.

Finally Benjamin grumbled, "You're gonna find them anyway." Hissing with pain as he moved, he dug in the front pocket of his jeans and extracted a white bundle, which he also threw. It landed beside the paint-covered packet.

Stan glanced at Sadie. "Hold that gun on him a second. If he moves, shoot him."

A grimly satisfied smile settled on her lips. "Gladly."

The chief holstered his own weapon, extracted a pair of rubber gloves from his jacket, and pulled them on. Holding the flashlight between his teeth, he squatted down and picked up the bundle, which became recognizable.

"It's an athletic sock," Mary Ann said. "The source of the white threads in the lamp?"

"That would be my guess." Liz nodded toward the paint-covered packet. "I have a feeling we'll find a matching one in there."

The sock had been knotted to keep the contents from falling out. Stan untied it and emptied something into his gloved hands. The tinkle of metal-on-metal sounded in the barn. He took the flashlight from his mouth and shone it on the items, which gleamed golden in the beam.

"Coins?" Liz looked at Mary Ann. "Why would they risk everything for a few old coins?"

Stan held one between a thumb and forefinger. "Unless I miss my guess, this coin is worth a lot more than face value."

"Which is?" Liz asked.

"Twenty bucks." He squinted to focus on the lettering and then burst out laughing. "You're not going to believe this. Do you know what this coin is called?"

Liz shook her head.

With a grin wide enough to reveal his molars, he said, "It's a Double Eagle."

Daylight found three of the Material Girls seated around Liz's kitchen table. Though Sadie had insisted she was fine, Liz and Mary

Ann had forced her to leave her farmhouse for the remainder of the night. They'd settled her in the Somewhere in Time Room, which Sarah had cleaned yesterday. Liz doubted that the other two women had gotten any more sleep than she had after their middle-of-the-night excitement, but even a few hours was better than none. Though they took turns yawning, Sadie looked much more like herself this morning.

The aroma of cheese and sausage wafted from the oven, a sign that Liz's breakfast casseroles were nearly done. Her laptop was open before her, and she clicked on another article her search had turned up.

"This is fascinating," she told her friends. "Double Eagles were first commissioned back in 1849 during the California Gold Rush and were made for nearly a hundred years afterward."

Sadie frowned. "They can't be all that valuable then. There must be thousands of them around. Why was that guy practically slobbering over the ten he had?"

"I think I know why," Liz said. "We didn't get a good look at them, but I have a feeling those ten were minted in 1933."

Mary Ann smoothed a lock of hair behind her ear. "I should probably know why that year's important, but I don't."

"It's the year FDR became president." Liz scanned the article and summarized. "He signed an executive order called the Gold Recall. Basically, it said no individual could hoard gold, but the interesting thing is he ordered the Philadelphia Mint to destroy all the gold coins that had just been minted, including the Double Eagles."

"Obviously, somebody didn't follow orders," Sadie said with a snort.

"All but one were melted down, or so they thought." She glanced over the top of her laptop. "But apparently some survived and found their way into the hands of a jeweler and scrap-metal dealer. When he died in 2013, his daughter and grandsons opened his safe deposit box, claiming they didn't know what was inside, though authorities noticed that the box had been rented six years after the dealer's death. They took the coins to the U.S. Treasury for authentication, and the government promptly seized them, insisting they'd been stolen from the Mint."

The timer on the oven dinged. "Keep reading," Mary Ann said. "I'll get the casseroles."

"Both the family and the government claim they own the coins." Lawyer Liz shook her head. In a high-stakes fight like this, lawsuits and appeals could continue forever. "I guess the battle is still going on, and the coins were moved to Fort Knox for safekeeping until somebody can figure out what to do with them."

"Apparently your fake singing group had an idea of their own." Mary Ann drew a beautifully browned casserole from the oven and slid it onto a trivet on the counter. "You said the government thought they'd melted all but one. What happened to that one?"

Liz scanned another article. "It was sold legally to King Farouk of Egypt for 7.6 million dollars."

Sadie slapped a hand on the table. "Holy moly! How much are those ten worth?"

"According to an article by the Associated Press after the latest trial, around eighty million dollars."

Awe crept over the older woman's features. "And to think I had half of them stashed in a paint can out in my toolshed."

Mary Ann returned to her chair. "Eighty million dollars is enough for our five conspirators to live quite comfortably under assumed names in another country."

"I'm kind of impressed with Gavin's foresight," Liz said. "He divided the coins and hid them in two places. That way if someone had found one stash, at least they wouldn't find them all."

Sadie scowled. "Too bad he told Benjamin that they were hidden at Louise's house. If he'd kept that to himself, she might still be alive."

Liz closed her laptop slowly. Everything they'd learned fit, but something still felt unfinished. How had all five of these men ended up at *her* inn? Had Gavin suggested it? Perhaps. And maybe Benjamin sent his sister because he didn't want to be associated with his partners-in-crime, yet wanted an excuse to meet with them here.

And there was still the matter of the hit-and-run accident that created the vacancies in the first place. Had Benjamin caused it? She had no problem believing it of him, but how could he have known the wedding party was coming here to stay?

Hopefully Stan would find something out when he questioned the suspects.

Liz left her friends serving themselves from one of the breakfast casseroles and took the other to the dining room. She was setting a pitcher of chilled orange juice on the table when Caleb Porter entered.

She greeted the young man with a cheerful, "Good morning."

"It *is* a good morning." The grin he gave her was more relaxed than any she had yet seen from him. "Your bed is a lot more comfortable than a quilt on top of a mound of hay."

"I'm glad to hear it." Holding the pitcher aloft and raising an eyebrow, she filled his glass when he nodded. "I know it's none of my business, but I can't help being curious. Have you made a decision?"

He took a seat and picked up the juice. "The decision was made days ago. I've never felt more at home or more myself than I have since we got to Pleasant Creek." He glanced toward the ceiling, where his parents' room lay. "I don't want to hurt Mother and Dad, but a man has to make up his own mind how to live."

Liz hesitated. Caleb was not her concern, but she felt a sense of responsibility for the young man since she'd given him the means to slip away from his parents.

"Would you listen to a little unasked-for advice?" When he nodded, she dropped into a chair opposite him. "I've only been in Pleasant Creek a short time, but one thing has become apparent to me. Amish people occasionally leave the faith, like my mother did. It's hard on them to give up the only lifestyle they've ever known, but it's even harder for someone who has grown up in our world to turn their backs on all the conveniences we take for granted." She shook her head. "I love my Amish relatives, and I admire their beliefs, but I don't think I could do it."

He held her gaze, unblinking. "I understand how difficult it will be. I really do. Maybe I'll fail. Maybe I won't be able to make the sacrifices. But I'm going to try." Sincerity rang in his voice. "And I mean to succeed."

Staring into his eyes, Liz believed he would.

Any reply she might have made went unsaid when his parents entered the room. While Caleb radiated peace, the older Porters looked dismal. The corners of Eunice's mouth sagged downward, pulling the rest of her features with them. Otis helped her to a chair with a firm grasp on her arm and then slumped despondently into his own.

Though she normally enjoyed the habit of taking breakfast with her guests, this morning she felt out of place in her own dining room. They remained silent while she served them, Eunice and Otis casting mournful stares across the table at their son, who dove into the casserole with gusto. Then she excused herself.

A pot of coffee waited for her back in the kitchen, but she needed something a bit stronger this morning. Biting back a yawn, she headed for the sitting room and a pod of espresso. She might even have a double.

In the rotunda she found a curious sight. Beans crouched alongside the staircase, his ears pointed forward, his muscles taut. Had he been a bird dog she would have said he was pointing. She started to ask what in the world he was doing, but then caught sight of a movement that made her snap her mouth shut.

Frank descended the stairs, his head and tail high. He moved with feline grace, almost regally, as though confident of his position not only in this house, but the world in general. From his position he could not have seen the bulldog hunkered down below.

Liz bit back a delighted chuckle as she anticipated the oncoming attack.

Frank's front paw left the bottom stair and touched the floor. Before his hind legs could follow, Beans pounced. Had she not seen the speed with which he flew forward she would not have believed it. Beans, who couldn't win a race with a garden snail, landed in front of Frank and clouted the cat's rump with one paw. With a startled yowl, Frank shot two feet straight up in the air. His feet were moving before they touched the ground, and he disappeared into the kitchen.

Liz dropped to the floor and gathered Beans in a hug.

"See, all you had to do was stand up for yourself. I told you so."

His head high, the bulldog headed after the cat, moving with what could almost be described as a prance.

Liz returned to the sitting room. While she waited for the machine to produce her double espresso, her thoughts wandered. Everything seemed to be tied up in a nice, neat bow. So why did she still feel like they'd missed something? Coffee hissed into her cup, and the aroma had a bracing effect on her thoughts. She just needed to lay everything out logically. Then it would probably all make sense, and she could dismiss this nagging sensation.

Benjamin and Gavin had worked together, which explained their connection. Check.

Two of the "Three Eagles" also lived in Radcliff. Check.

Phil—really Ed Collins—lived in Fort Knox, which was near Radcliff. Check.

They all hung out at the same pub, which is how they met each other. *Hmmm.* Three professional government employees frequented the same pub as two thugs? That seemed like a big coincidence. Unless Radcliff was so small there weren't many places to choose from.

The hissing stopped and the last of the water sputtered out of the machine. Liz took her cup to the sofa, where she pulled out her cell phone. She really had no knowledge about the location or size of towns in Kentucky. In the map application she punched in *Radcliff, KY*. The town appeared as a small blob on the map, slightly south of Fort Knox. A quick search told her the distance between the two was less than two miles. So the five conspirators connecting at a local establishment was entirely possible.

Out of curiosity, she used her fingers on the phone's screen to shrink the map. Benjamin had grown up in Frankfort, where Betty still lived. She located the state capitol on the map. East of Louisville on Interstate 64, just past—

Liz sucked in a breath. The name of the town blazed from the screen like a glowing coal. Her espresso forgotten, she leaped off the couch and dashed from the sitting room to the desk in the foyer. Hands shaking, she unlocked the drawer and pulled out her reservation calendar. Heart pounding inside her rib cage, she located the reservation for the wedding party. Yes, her memory was correct. They lived in Shelbyville, Kentucky, which lay just a few miles west of Frankfort.

Her fingers trembled so badly she could barely punch the query into her cell phone. When she found the *Shelbyville Standard*, it took only a moment of searching the archives before she came across the article she sought. A bicycler was the victim of a hit-and-run accident on Route 60, not far from the Franklin County line. Another search led her to a nearly identical article in another newspaper. She scanned the details, a dreadful certainty settling over her.

Stan thinks he has the whole bunch in custody. But he doesn't. Because one of them is here, at my inn!

"There you are."

At the sound of the voice, Liz whirled.

And faced the sixth conspirator.

21

"Uh, good morning," Liz managed to stammer.

Betty wore her coat and held one of her hard-shelled suitcases in her hand. "I hope you didn't plan on me for breakfast. With everything that's happened I don't think my poor stomach could handle a meal."

"Uh." Thoughts whirling, Liz glanced at the desk for anything that might be used as a defensive weapon if the need arose. Nothing. "It's a breakfast casserole." A lame answer, but her mind was busy trying to make sense of her suspicions. *I could be wrong. I* pray *I'm wrong.* But deep inside, she knew she'd stumbled on an awful truth.

"Delicious, I'm sure, but I'm afraid I'll have to pass. I must get home. Would you mind helping me with the rest of my bags?"

Betty retreated into the rotunda, where two more suitcases rested at the foot of the stairs. Liz followed at a cautious distance.

"I—I'm surprised you're leaving so soon," she said.

"That police chief did say I was free to go," Betty reminded her.

"Yes." Liz swallowed against a desert-dry throat. "Yes, he did. I just thought since your brother was arrested last night, you might want to stay in the area until he's released from the hospital."

"Hospital?" Her nostrils flared, and the suitcase fell to the floor from nerveless fingers. "Has Benjamin been injured?"

She didn't know. Of course she wouldn't.

"He'll recover," Liz assured her. "He was shot while robbing one of my friends and holding her hostage."

Liz spared a hope that Sadie and Mary Ann would stay in the safety of the kitchen. On the other hand, maybe she should raise her voice loud enough to be heard. If they detected the tension in her voice, they might call Stan.

Betty gasped. "Oh my dear, that's terrible. I am so sorry."

Perhaps Liz was hearing through the filter of her suspicions, but Betty's sympathy lacked sincerity. In fact, her expression had taken on a narrow-eyed shrewdness that made Liz want to squirm.

Betty cleared her throat. "Has Benjamin said anything to the police? I mean, has he confessed to anything?"

Was there a note of worry in the question?

"I don't know," Liz answered honestly.

She should let her go. Pick up the suitcases and help her to her car, and then call Stan the moment she drove away. But what if she disappeared completely? What if Liz's suspicions were true, and she let a killer escape?

Betty tilted her head and studied Liz with a hard stare. "My dear, you look distraught. Is something wrong?"

Keep your mouth shut, Liz. Leave this to the police.

She ignored the whisper of logic. "To be honest, I've just discovered something that is kind of worrying. I never realized how close Frankfort is to Shelbyville."

Betty became still, but she did not take her gaze from Liz's. "And why is that worrying?"

"Because I've been trying to figure out how the inn just happened to have rooms available at the same time as Louise Younger's auction and Gavin's release from jail. How would Benjamin have known about the bride and groom's wedding when they live in Shelbyville, and he lives ninety miles south of there?"

The woman made no answer, but her lips pressed into a tight line.

Liz watched her closely. "But when I saw that Franklin County and Shelby County are right next to each other, I realized that the newspapers probably report some of the same local news. Sure enough, I found an account of the accident in the *State Journal*, which is Frankfort's paper."

Betty's eyes narrowed. "I don't like your tone, Ms. Eckardt."

Tension stretched Liz's nerves to near-breaking, but she couldn't stop now.

"The article said there were no witnesses to the actual accident, but someone came upon it right after it happened. That person reported seeing a car speeding away from the scene. A black Buick with its license plate covered."

"I can hardly believe my ears," Betty said, though her tone sounded shrill in Liz's ears. "Do you know how many black Buicks there are on the road?"

Liz went on. "I found another article in the Shelbyville paper, this one dated a week before. The bride and groom's engagement announcement, including their plans for a private family wedding in Pleasant Creek. And where else would the bridal party stay, but at the Olde Mansion Inn? Since your brother knew Gavin, he must have known he was from this area. But you told me you hadn't seen Benjamin in a long time. So I guess the question is, how did Benjamin find out about that wedding, and when did he have enough time to discover the groom's habit of a daily early morning bicycle ride?"

From the slight widening of Betty's eyes, Liz knew she'd hit her mark.

"Oh, no." A sob choked Betty's words. "I must not have mentioned the fact that dear Benjamin did come to see me on his way up here. He borrowed my car. You don't suppose he used *my* car to run over that poor young man, do you?"

Had the undercurrents in the conversation not been so tense, Liz might have laughed. The woman was throwing her own "dear brother" under the bus.

Liz forced a smile, which probably looked more like a grimace. "I suppose if you keep old newspapers around—"

"I do," Betty said quickly.

"Then maybe Benjamin saw the announcement at your house. I'll tell Chief Houghton what I've uncovered and leave everything to him." She made a point of dropping her gaze to the suitcases. "I'm sure he'll have a lot of questions for you about the incident."

Betty's face went completely white. Her eyes flickered around the rotunda. Looking for an escape route?

Suddenly Betty shoved a hand into her coat pocket. In the next instant, Liz found herself facing the barrel of a gun.

She sucked in a breath and held it, her heart pounding a wild rhythm.

"That's quite enough. You won't be making any calls, Ms. Eckardt. I can't allow that."

Alarms buzzed in her ears so loudly she could barely make out the woman's words.

What was I thinking? Why didn't I just let her go and call Stan?

A nightmare. That's what this was. Liz would have pinched her arm in an effort to wake herself, but fear held her frozen in place.

Please keep the Porters in the dining room, and Sadie and Mary Ann safely in the kitchen.

Betty's arrogant voice traveled up the stairway and echoed off the rotunda's domed ceiling. "I hate that circumstances have led us to this, truly I do. In the meantime, I do not intend—"

Whatever Betty didn't intend was lost in the skirmish that followed. The sound of toenails scrabbling on hardwood, along with a fearful feline yowling, broke through the ringing in Liz's ears. Frank shot into the room from the kitchen doorway, Beans in hot pursuit. The terrified cat launched itself into the air and landed, claws bared, on his owner's arm. Betty screamed as the bulldog, in a totally un-Beans-like move, hurled himself after the cat, knocking the woman to the floor.

The gun went off.

The explosion seemed to shatter the air, echoing through all three stories of the rotunda. It was quickly followed by the sounds of screams and running feet throughout the inn. The gun skittered across the floor, knocked from Betty's grasp. Liz lunged for the gun and plowed into Betty, who had the same goal. Her slender frame no match for Betty's considerable bulk, Liz was hurled sideways and landed on the floor with a thud that knocked the breath out of her. As she gasped to fill her deprived lungs, Beans planted his shivering, whimpering body against her side.

Betty scrambled across the floor. A figure dashed into the rotunda from the foyer, leaped over Liz, and literally dove toward the gun.

Stan? But where—

Still gasping for breath, Liz's oxygen-deprived brain barely registered Betty crawling on hands and knees after the gun. The police chief reached the weapon an instant before her, planted a foot on it, and pointed his own revolver at her.

"That's enough, Ms. Lewis."

Stan's commanding voice filled the room and sent relief flooding through Liz. People filed through the dining room doorway. Mary Ann and Sadie hurried to Liz's side, while the Porters stood gaping at Betty huddled on the floor.

Liz threw her arms around Beans and hugged him for all he was worth. "What a good boy!" she sobbed. "Such a good boy!"

22

Liz, with a quilt wrapped around her shivering shoulders, perched on the sitting room sofa with her friends on either side.

In a facing chair, Stan studied her with professional concern. "Are you sure you don't want me to call a doctor?"

Mary Ann put an arm around Liz's shoulders and hugged. "It might not hurt. Just to be on the safe side."

"They could give you something to calm you down," Sadie added.

"I'm fine," she told them for the third time. "I've had a shock, that's all. I mean, how often does a person have a gun pointed in her face? It's unsettling."

A slight grin appeared on Stan's face. "It's happened to me a number of times. Sort of goes with the job."

"Your job, not mine." But Liz gave a small laugh, which helped to relieve some of the tension. The uncontrollable shivering slowed. "What I want to know is how you knew to come when you did."

"I was coming to pick up Betty and take her in for questioning since we have her brother. I needed to make sure she didn't know more than she was saying. When I approached the inn, I saw you through the window. Your posture was so tense and stiff I knew something was wrong, so I cracked open the door quietly and heard part of the conversation. That's when I realized my suspect had cornered you." His shoulders heaved with a humorless laugh. "Or maybe it was the other way around."

"But why?" Liz shook her head. "What made you suspect her?"

"Do you think you're the only one with access to the Internet and the ability to put two and two together?" His expression became stern. "You shouldn't have confronted her. She could have killed you, you know. She's killed before."

Mary Ann's arm tightened around Liz's shoulders. "Did she kill Gavin?"

Stan shook his head. "No, Benjamin killed Gavin after they argued about the location of the stolen coins. Betty killed Louise Younger."

Liz and her friends all gasped.

"How do you know that?" Sadie asked.

"Because I have three eagles in my jail who are singing like songbirds." He smiled at the play on words. "They're pointing fingers all over the place. Laying everything out. Conspiracy. Theft. Murder." He leaned forward and planted his elbows on his knees. "All three insist they kept their end of the bargain. They stole the Double Eagles six weeks ago and replaced them with duplicates so the theft wasn't noticed right away. They met Benjamin at a pub in Radcliff, and he was their contact to fence the coins. As for Gavin." Stan shook his head and gave a sad laugh. "Poor Gavin was a convenient dupe. He happened to be hanging out at the bar after work with Benjamin when Mardel approached him, and Gavin inserted himself into the deal. He insisted he could hide the coins somewhere they could never be found until the heat cooled. And he did."

"In Louise's house," Mary Ann said sadly.

Stan nodded. "His mistake was in telling Benjamin that he'd stashed the coins at his aunt's house. Benjamin made contact with a buyer as promised. But in the meantime, Gavin got arrested. The jail's records show Benjamin visiting him, but recordings of their conversation were cryptic. Benjamin asked where he'd put his *pets* while Gavin was away, and Gavin assured him that they were *secure*." Stan snorted a humorless laugh. "Secure. Odd word to use for pets, or at least that's what the guards down there thought when they reviewed the tape."

Liz glanced at Beans, who lay snoring on the hearth in front of the fire Sadie had started when Liz's shivering began. He'd saved her life.

"So Benjamin made a deal with some very nasty people who wanted those Double Eagles. When he realized how much trouble he was in, he did what he always does. He called his big sister to get him out of a bind. Betty took matters into her own hands and drove up to Fort Wayne to search Louise Younger's house. Unfortunately, Ms. Younger came home and surprised her and . . ." He didn't have to finish the sentence.

Liz resisted the temptation to picture the confrontation. "But Betty turned over the lamp and told you where to find Benjamin. Why would she do that to her own brother?"

"To cover her tracks," Stan replied confidently. "If I were to make a guess, I'd say she *did* speak with her brother when she went out to the cabin yesterday. He confessed to killing Gavin and told her he had half the coins. She wanted him to hand them over to her and he refused. That shook her trust in her ability to manipulate him. She knew we'd catch him eventually, and she'd rather implicate him in murder than go to prison herself." He shrugged. "Part of that's conjecture, but I have a strong hunch I'm right. And that the feds will get the truth out of both brother and sister in good time."

"Let's hope so," Mary Ann said.

"You feeling better now?" Stan asked Liz.

Her head was spinning with all the information he'd relayed, but she no longer felt cold and shaky. "I am," she replied, and then smiled. "As I said I would."

"Good." He slapped his hands on his thighs and stood. "Then I'll leave you in these ladies' capable hands." With a nod at Sadie and Mary Ann, he strode from the room.

Liz glanced at her watch. "Do you realize it's only ten o'clock? I feel like I've been chained behind a truck and dragged through mountain country."

Sadie patted her on the knee. "You've been through a lot."

"We all have," Mary Ann said. "I think we deserve to take the rest of the morning off. Let's pretend like we're Beans and have a nap."

Liz settled further into the cushy sofa, completely comfortable between her friends. "That's a wonderful idea."

A few days later, Liz measured out a square of bright Christmas fabric and marked it with chalk. "This new area rug gives the shop a bright, cheerful feel, don't you think?" The Material Girls stood around the newly refinished worktable in Sew Welcome's craft area, cutting squares for their holiday quilt.

"It looks great." Sadie peered at the rug. "I could almost be glad the whole thing happened."

Mary Ann and Liz paused in their work to give her a horrified look.

She shrugged. "Well, except for the stabbings and the shootings and the robbery and all that."

Liz chuckled. "Yes, except for those things."

Several neat piles of squares lay in the center of the table. They hadn't been able to get any more of the snowman fabric, but Liz liked this Christmas tree design even better.

"How is Frank doing?" she asked as she laid her square on top of the others.

When Betty Lewis had been led away in handcuffs, naturally she'd left her cat behind. Liz had been faced with a dilemma. What to do with Frank? Though she liked cats, Beans had apparently decided to seek retribution every time the two came in contact, and Frank had taken to hiding beneath the dining room buffet. That was no life for a cat. Liz could not bear to turn an animal in to the pound. Sadie solved the problem when she volunteered to take him home with her. This surprised everyone, given her utter devotion to Beans and the cat's history of tormenting him.

"He's not Frank anymore." Sadie stretched the bright red-and-green border fabric across the measurement guide. "Stupid name for a cat. No animal of mine will ever have a people name."

"What do you call him?" Mary Ann asked.

"Dipsy Doodle."

Liz laughed. "What a name."

Sadie shrugged. "It fits, and he doesn't care. He's settled right in. Terrorizes the squirrels, and my toolshed hasn't seen a mouse since he arrived."

"Oh, do you make the poor thing stay outside?" kindhearted Mary Ann asked.

"Make him? He loves it. But I bring him inside at night, and he sleeps with me. I'll probably keep him inside more as the weather gets colder, but for now it's still warm enough for him to be outside." She grinned. "Got my own little furry hot-water bottle for cold winter nights."

The bells on the shop door jingled, and they all looked up to see a young woman enter. Her plain dress and Kapp identified her as Amish. She stepped into the shop and came to a halt, her gaze settling on Liz. Though she looked vaguely familiar, Liz couldn't place her.

Until she spoke.

"Hello. I hoped you'd be here. I wanted to thank you."

In a flash, Liz recognized her. "Leah!"

She dropped the scissors and hurried across the room to gather the girl in a hug.

"I came home." A smile lit the lovely features. "Thanks to you."

The story of Leah Schwartz's return had swept through the community. When Asa and Viola had arrived at Leah's apartment in Indianapolis, there was no one home. Thank goodness Liz had thought to mention the name of the grocery store she'd seen on the young woman's name tag. The Schwartzes' driver had used his phone to locate the store and taken them there. Apparently the reunion had been tearful and joyful, and had resulted in an ecstatic homecoming.

"I'm so glad," Liz told her.

Mary Ann and Sadie joined them, each giving the girl a welcoming embrace.

"You've made your family very happy." Mary Ann beamed.

"I am happy too," the girl assured them. "I will take the classes when they are offered next year and make my commitment to the church."

"I heard there's to be another new church member in those classes as well." Sadie waggled her eyebrows. "And maybe we'll have a wedding in the fall."

Mary Ann tilted her head and gave her a disapproving look. "That's just speculation. Don't gossip, Sadie."

"Who, me?" The brassy woman placed a hand on her chest, eyebrows arched over guileless blue eyes.

Though she was often privy to local chitchat, Liz hadn't heard this one. "You can't make a statement like that and leave me hanging. Who are you talking about?"

"Caleb Porter, of course." Sadie folded her arms across her chest, clearly pleased to pass on a bit of news to a fresh set of ears. "He and Anna Beachy rode home together from the young people singing last week. You know, when the unmarried Amish gather to sing hymns together after church."

A sure sign of courtship. Liz had not seen the young man since the morning he'd assured her he would succeed in his determination to become Amish, though Eunice had called a few days ago to book a room over the Christmas holiday so they could visit with their son. She sounded resigned to having an Amish child.

"I must go," Leah told her. "I left Mutter at the store."

Liz looped an arm through hers. "I'll walk you out."

In the foyer, Leah hesitated before opening the front door. "I think about Gavin often." The statement sounded more like a confession than anything.

"That's understandable," Liz assured her. "After all, you were in love with him at one time."

"I thought I was." The girl shook her head, her expression sad. "Now I'm not sure. But even if I didn't truly love him, I didn't want anything bad to happen to him. Or to his aunt." She searched Liz's face. "What will happen to the person who killed them?"

"People," Liz corrected. "A woman killed Louise, and her brother killed Gavin. After accusing each other for several days, they finally both confessed."

"They will go to prison?"

Liz nodded. "Definitely. Along with a few others."

Once Benjamin Baggett realized he was being accused not only by the three Fort Knox employees, but also by his own sister, he tried to cut a deal. He laid out the whole plan for the federal prosecutor, including the identity of the mystery coin dealer, who he fingered as the hostile "Joe" who'd demanded to speak with Gavin the night of the homecoming football game.

Leah closed her eyes and drew a breath. "I will pray for them all."

The words plucked at Liz's heartstrings. That was a beautiful thing about the Amish. They wished no one ill will, even those who caused them pain. Maybe especially those.

She gathered the girl in an embrace. "I will too."

When she'd closed the door behind Leah Schwartz, Liz's gaze fell on Beans. Stretched out on his rug, the dog was enjoying his favorite pastime—a nap. A soft snore rose from his smooshed-up nose.

Liz whispered in the lowest voice she could produce. "Want a treat?"

He was on his feet in an instant.

"I thought so."

Laughing, she headed for the kitchen and the jar that contained his favorite chewy morsels. All-natural and guaranteed to appeal to canine tastes, they cost a fortune. That was okay with her. Beans might be the laziest dog on the planet, but nothing was too good for her canine hero.

Liz leaned down to stroke Beans's head. Her heart warmed as the sounds of happy chatter from Sew Welcome drifted through the inn.

Good friends, like the ones she'd made here in Pleasant Creek, were worth more than all the gold in Fort Knox.